WHY THE BIRDS FLY BACK

WHY THE BIRDS FLY BACK

AKOSUA HARVEY

STIRRED STORIES

Copyright © 2025 by Akosua Harvey
Published by Stirred Stories.
All rights reserved.

This is a work of fiction. People, places, and scenarios are either a product of the author's imagination or used fictitiously.

ISBN 9798990856936
First edition: October 2025

ATTENTION SCHOOLS AND BUSINESSES:
Stirred Stories books are available at a discount for bulk purchase. Complete the general inquiries form at www.stirredstories.com/contact.

Cover and interior design by Zina Fattah

*To the Harveys, the Briskers, the Johnsons and Monroes,
the Sealeys, the Nurses, and the Hughes.
A special thanks to Aunt Marybell and Uncle VanDyke.
Of the past and towards the future, I am because you are.*

Marissa Lanae
Jeremy Cole
Jacob Cole
Michael Cole "Tre" Swallowtail III
Marvin and Yonna
Michael Cole Swallowtail Jr. and Sarah
Aunt Marybell and Uncle VanDyke
Michael Cole Swallowtail Sr.
Gizelle

Marsha Claire
Swallowtail

GLOSSARY

Clairaudience

gift of hearing—ability to hear things others can't

Claircognizance

gift of knowing—extreme intuition

Clairsentience

gift of feeling—ability to feel things beyond normal perception

Clairvoyance

gift of sight—ability to see into the past or future

CONTENTS

PART I
CAGED

I

BIRDS ARE SUCH STRANGE CREATURES. *They have all this sky, all them wings and still don't know how to fly away. And when they do finally figure it out … they take off just to come right on back. Insanity! It's a waste of potential if you ask me—spending all their time perched on top of Aunt Marybell's pool screen, not traveling the world. I mean, God put all these beautiful things here just to beg questions, and these birds decide to just sit there, okay with only knowing the things they know right here, right now. I don't get it! If I were a bird, I wouldn't waste one second. Every day, I'd fly somewhere new, somewhere farther and farther away from Ocala, Florida. Tomorrow, I'd drop a penny and feather off the Leaning Tower of Pisa to see what Galileo was talking about. On Tuesday, I'd rest in the healing waters of Lake Tana, then take off into the permanent rainbow over Blue Nile Falls. I'd gaze over the Andes, find treasure in the Bermuda Triangle. I'd never stop looking for everything this world has to offer. Because here, all I have is this pool screen and these dang on birds reminding me that I can't.*

"Marsha! Watch out!" squeaked a voice in the distance.

Helplessly yanked out of her daydream, Marsha Claire Swallowtail braced herself for the inevitable.

SPLASHHHH!

As he had done at least once every day for the entire summer they spent in Ocala, her older brother, Jeremy, managed to sneak under her pool float undetected. With one swift motion, he lifted the side of her float and dunked her in the water before she could even plug her nose.

Marsha hated getting dunked more than any other way her brother chose to torment her. She tried everything she could think of to avoid it—concocting plans, staging diversions. One time she even jumped right onto his back where she thought he couldn't reach her. Jeremy simply sacrificed himself and they both went plunging backwards into the water.

Marsha couldn't turn to Marissa, the oldest Swallowtail child. All Marissa would do was tell him to stop, which he would, but only long enough to devise some other painfully irksome method of harassment. So Marsha resorted to today's most shameless act of bribing Jacob, her youngest sibling, with a quarter to warn her when Jeremy got too close. She knew this was a risky move—Jacob would do anything for Marsha, but Jeremy would surely go after him as soon as he realized who snitched. What kind of big sister put her baby brother in harm's way?

Well you know what, the kind that was tired! Today was their last day in Ocala, and after all of the boredom, annoyance, and loneliness this summer away had brought, the only thing Marsha wanted to do was wallow in her daydreams until they landed her home in Accokeek, Maryland.

Welp, it turns out bribing a four-year-old didn't cut her losses after all. Her world tumbled around her, swooshing and swashing in distorted streaks of light while she sunk in disarray. The shallow disappointment seemed like the theme of Marsha's summer.

"Jacob! Your ass is grass!" Jeremy yelled as he rampaged through the water in pursuit.

Jacob screamed and ran to seek safety in Marissa's arms, but Jeremy, who seemed to have doubled in size over the summer, managed to mangle them both into the water.

SWOOSH ... SPLASHHHHHHHHH!

Jacob let out another shriek, pinning Marsha to the bottom of the pool beneath her guilt. She sat there on the jagged floor, listening to their laughs and screams while the wispy ends of her cornrowed hair brushed against her cheeks.

I wonder if they would notice if I never came back up.

Pressing the soles of her feet into the roughness, Marsha burrowed to the surface of the water. Between the haze of chlorine, the water sloshing out of her ears, and the bright, white Florida sun, it took her a few moments to fully come to her senses. Jacob was crying and Marissa was giggling, gently scooping him out of the water.

Marissa never got upset with Jeremy. She never got upset with any of them. She wasn't that type of big sister. She was the type to play along with every joke and imaginary story, and take responsibility for every mistake, even if it wasn't her own. She was their liaison, the interpreter of a parent's vigilant love and a child's longing for freedom. She was adored by everyone who met her, but no one adored her more than her siblings. Even Jeremy seemed to submit to her unconditional love. Marissa looked equally as much like her mother as she did her father, taking both of their best physical and emotional traits. She had her father's silky hair and solid frame. She carried the Swallowtail family's strong presence and innate love for every little creation like a regal gown passed to her from the ancestors. She had her mother's deep eyes, just brown enough to tell. Her sharp cupid's bow, perfected by honest thoughts, fretless comedy, and intimate connections, stood out against thick, burgundy lips. The Swallowtail family had their troubles, as every family does, but Marissa was the joy, responsibility, and beauty that held it all together. At seventeen, Marissa Lanae Swallowtail was the first born any parent would pray for, and the model woman Marsha could only hope to become.

"You're okay Jacob, it's only a little water," Marissa soothed, holding his head against her chest. "Jeremy, that wasn't cool. He coulda banged his head!" She paused to wipe the droplets, heavy with chlorine, from Jacob's hairline before any more reached the redness of his tearful eyes. "If you were smart, you woulda thrown us in the deep end!" she joked.

"Next time," Jeremy said, bucking at Jacob with a ghoulish grin.

Jacob squealed and tightened his bony ankles around Marissa's waist. This time, it was more about the performance than the fear.

"God had no business making that boy so big is all I'm saying!" Aunt Marybell commented as the screen door screeched open. A phone was pinned between her shrugged shoulder and right ear, with the landline's coiled wire stretching through the threshold before disappearing into the home. "Let me call you back after I get these children together. Jeremy Cole, I know that wasn't you I heard using that language in my house! And what is all this screaming?"

"Technically I'm not *in* the house," Jeremy contested, only to be met by the silencing threat of his great-aunt's glare.

"We were just playing," Marissa explained, quickly defusing the situation with grace beyond her years. She waded Jacob over to the curvy edge of the pool so he could find more sanctuary in the tall, sturdy, old woman.

"Jeremy … *sniff* … dunked … *sniff* … me and I … *sniff* … got wader in my eaws," Jacob wined.

"Yo Jacob, if you plug your nose and blow you can push it all out!"

"Jeremy, hush! Why you gotta be so nasty all the time?" scolded Aunt Marybell. "Jacob, baby, come on in the house so I can get you cleaned up. The rest of you too, your daddy should be here any minute."

Those were the words Marsha had been waiting to hear all day. Filled with excitement, she dove to the pool ladder and darted towards the door. Just like that, the race to the bathroom commenced. Unlike their home in Accokeek—a three-level townhouse with one bathroom for the boys, and another for the girls nestled between bedrooms on the second floor— the single-floored Floridian-style house in Ocala held only enough space for two bathrooms total. One was connected to the master bedroom and was unspokenly off-limits to all of the children except Jacob. The three oldest siblings shared the guest bathroom way down at the end of the far hall. One bathroom to brush your teeth. One bathroom to shower. One bathroom to escape to after Aunt Marybell makes her savory-sweet baked beans. One more reason to despise Ocala.

Marsha threw her towel around her shoulders like a cape and zoomed past Aunt Marybell into the yellow, adobe home, ducking under the telephone wire. She glided through the maze of China displays and plastic-covered dining chairs that surrounded the carved wooden dinner table, being sure not to slip on her pruned wet feet. Great-Uncle VanDyke silently sat in his La-Z-Boy as he always did, blankly staring into the painting above the piano that gave his name its legend. She brushed a kiss atop his head as she skirted by.

"Marsha, I call dibs!" Jeremy yelled from the distance, normally a mutually respected automatic win, but Marsha had a contingency plan. All she had to do to solidify the win was get to the bathroom first.

A side-step into the kitchen. A twist into the hall. Marsha could see the finish line. Sprinting down the corridor, she could hear Marissa and Jeremy behind her. She charged into the bathroom and locked the door before Beauty and the Beast even reached the kitchen.

A few moments later, "Marsha! I said I called dibs!" Jeremy yelled, punctuating his demand with three bangs on the bathroom door.

"My clothes were already in here!" Marsha said, solidifying an automatic win.

Every day at 10 A.M. sharp, after breakfast at eight, and reading at nine, Aunt Marybell sent the Swallowtail children outside to play in the pool. Marsha hated it. It always came at the wrong time in her book, the chlorine always stained her eyes red, and Jeremey had uninterrupted time to torment her. Marissa tried to help Aunt Marybell to convince Marsha that sibling time was important, but Marsha wrote it off as some type of pre-fulfilled karma.

Today, Marsha stayed back for a few moments to "use the bathroom." Aunt Marybell always locked the screen door for privacy to help Uncle VanDyke get dressed for the day, so she knew her stuff would be safe. Just before going outside, Marsha snuck her pre-prepared bag of toiletries and folded stack of clothes into the guest bathroom. That way, if she missed her cue, she could play her card.

"That's cheating, Marsha!" shouted Marissa.

Jeremy pounded on the door again. Marsha rushed to turn on the water.

"Huh? Can't hear you over the shower!"

Pressing her ear against the door, she heard Marissa kiss her lips and coax Jeremy back down the hall. *At least this plan worked.*

The scent of lavender pure-castile soap rose with the steam to over-power the chlorine. After bathing herself, Marsha poured a few drops of the soap onto her bright orange one-piece bathing suit and scrubbed until the heavy stench disappeared there too.

After drying off, moisturizing, and brushing her teeth, Marsha turned to look at herself in the large, full-length mirror leaning on the bathroom wall. Aunt Marybell was a reserved woman with an eccentric style. Her home was filled with art, photos, artifacts, and plants from all over the world. The most stunning pieces, however, were the mirrors. They were the centerpiece of every room. This one flaunted a gold, textured frame with small leaves to give the illusion of a twisted branch. Marsha gazed at her own abstract frame standing between its borders, her dark, red ochre skin shining out like the pit against the olive painted walls.

Skin, Dad.

Eyes, Mom.

Lips, Mom.

Shoulders, Dad.

Big-bonededness, Dad.

No curves ... a genetic mutation.

"Today's affirmations ..." she said quietly to herself as she closed her eyes, "I have smooth skin, a beautiful brain, and today, I'm taking them both back to Maryland, back to where they belong." Opening her eyes, Marsha smiled big in the mirror, took a breath, and allowed herself to feel hopeful for the first time all summer.

II

Yonna Swallowtail rode silently next to her husband, trying her hardest to loosen herself from their tie so she could, for a moment, feel feelings of her own. She needed to examine her own emotions about everything that had occurred, but this was a task easier said than done. Marvin and Yonna were a unit, intertwined by more than commitment or obligation, responsibility or trust. They were united by spirit. By care. By intention. When he moved, she felt the ripple and rode the waves with expertise. When she shifted, he became both her water and her raft. It was the deepest, truest love she had ever experienced. A love that created a space for Marvin to be confident in his mistakes and Yonna to soften into her nature. Their love had grown to observe rather than correct. Support rather than coddle. They both learned to live in love better this way.

This is the way their love had thrived for two decades now, so this was far from the first wrong decision she'd watched him make. It was the first, however, that directly affected their children. As a matter of fact, she didn't care much about how it affected anyone else besides their children. She knew their feelings would be hurt, but what worried her more was how it would jeopardize their entire relationship. Their bond was so far from what she'd had with her father, and so indicative of the bond Marvin had with his. Marsha in particular, as shrewd and cerebral as she was, still looked at her father the way young children look at superheroes. Marvin's tie to his babies was the single most important thing to him, and without saying a thing, Yonna had watched him push it closer and closer to a burning flame.

Guilt. When the smoke cleared and she finally felt herself, it was all guilt.

Marvin inched their midnight black Cadillac slowly through the tricky streets of Ocala. He inaudibly mouthed each street name—Pine Ave., Pine Street, Pine Road—focusing more than necessary to mask the dread lingering in his mind. Just three weeks earlier, Marvin felt like the world, once sand falling between his fingers, finally held like clay in the palm of his hands. The plan had been to drop the children off at his Aunt Marybell's house before heading to Key West to celebrate his and Yonna's wedding anniversary. They'd only been there for a few days before his twin brother Michael Cole Swallowtail III, who everyone called "Tre," visited him in a dream. He appeared hollow and ghostly looking, standing at the base of a large oak tree wearing a dastardly scorn. His eyes, pinned to his tether, sunk like a coffin in a grave. Marvin remained stoic as he always had. Dreams like this weren't new to him, and neither was his brother's look. In fact, it was the only way he knew his brother, disgusted at him— at his own DNA.

Suddenly, vine-like ropes of fire fell from a thick branch of the tree and clawed themselves down Tre's body. They began to pull Tre towards a branch where a whirlpool of dark nothingness opened at its base. Marvin rushed to his rescue, but the fiery vines burst into the air, thrusting Marvin to the ground. The last thing he saw was his twin's pleading eyes fading into the black. The next morning, Tre called him with news that changed more than just the anniversary plans.

He and Yonna first left Ocala just after the twins' father had died. Marsha was still a baby and the growing family didn't really have a plan. It took some time, but together, they molded their life into the sculpture of success Marvin only once dreamed of. They started a property management company and quickly became one of the most sought-after contractors in southern Maryland. More importantly to Marvin, he established a life for himself apart from Tre, a life better than Tre's. The rivalry began the moment they were born, when just a few minutes' difference meant Tre got their father's name, and Marvin didn't. The identical boys had since grown into mountainous men, boasting their indigenous heritage with broad shoulders and deep, rust-colored skin. While their only physical difference was the small, crescent-shaped birthmark outlining the underside of Marvin's right eye, their personalities were paradoxical. Their father had always said, "Tre gon' risk take, Marv gon' calculate," and according to Marvin, the risk was never worth the reward. After years of cleaning up all of "the risk's" messes, Marvin wanted to keep "the risk" as far away from him and his family as he could.

Now, over a decade after leaving, Tre had mustered up the only two things that could have brought Marvin back. First, there was the land. An old family rumor claimed their family owned forty-seven acres of land just on the boundary of the town, along the National Forest. It was their father's dying wish to get the deed to the land, but for some reason, he was never able to. Apparently a housing development was attempting to obtain the land thinking it was city property, and, Tre being Tre, made a bunch of enemies at the city council meeting about it. With a deed nowhere to be found, the city couldn't prove they or anyone else actually owned the land. They put the project on hold for three months. Then, the park system petitioned to halt the project indefinitely because of the portion of the land shared by the National Forest. The city granted an extra three months' extension, six months total. Still, the Swallowtails didn't have much time. Once more, Marvin was going to have to clean up Tre's mess for the sake of the family.

Then, there was the dream. Marvin had seen death on Tre, just like he had seen it on their mother and their father. As was the case with their parents, he didn't know when the moment would come, but he knew it was coming and Tre wasn't taking it seriously enough. A "little cancer?" Who says that about cancer? Nonetheless, Tre had no one. Aside from their father, Tre had blown to shreds every other valuable relationship he had ever formed. Until now, Marvin couldn't understand why their old man had kept giving Tre chance after chance. But Marvin now realized that, at the very least, he had a duty to be there if his brother's time was really up.

Marvin thought it was the right thing to hide the details and let the children enjoy their summer with Aunt Marybell. When he shared the plan with Yonna, he saw the doubt on her face though she nodded in agreement, and he told himself that after a few weeks everything would be straightened out. In the meantime, if he omitted the truth, essentially nobody would have to worry but him, and he had known worry for as long as he had known his own name.

But omission quickly turned into deceit. He lied to Marissa when she asked how the Key West beaches were. He lied to Jeremy when he asked about football tryouts back in Maryland. He lied to Marsha, time and time and time again, whenever she spoke about her excitement to go home. His baby girl was never quiet about her feelings. And now he had to tell his children the truth, that Ocala would be their new home, and their father, the person who they should trust and depend on more than anyone else, was a liar.

"Damnit!" he cursed, as he completed a turn onto Pine Street. "Pine Street, Pine Ave., Pine every got-damned thing!"

Yonna laced her fingers into his and squeezed until he let out a deep, surrendering sigh.

"Do you remember when Tre and I got in that fight at school?" Marvin asked a long moment later as he pulled into a driveway to turn the sedan around.

"Yeah, I remember. I don't know what you were more afraid of, getting suspended or your dad finding out."

"Huh," Marvin chuckled. "Definitely Dad. You know how he was about his namesake."

"*Namesakes* ... You got your daddy's name too, baby."

Marvin grunted.

"What brought that to mind?" Yonna continued, ignoring his reaction.

"Well, I knew when we only got detention that Dad spoke to Principal Drake and had him pull some strings, so whatever punishment we avoided was waiting for us when we got home. I kept playing the scene over and over in my head. You know, walking through the door and he's just standing there. I was so distracted. I think this is the same exact wrong turn I made that day. "

"I see." And again, guilt crept into the forefront of Yonna's mind.

Silence settled around them as they made the turn onto Pine Lane and stayed as they approached the cul-de-sac where most of Marvin's childhood memories were formed.

"So what did your dad end up doing?"

"He sat us down and reminded us what family was."

And with that, Yonna understood.

III

It had been six weeks and two days since Marsha had last seen her parents, the longest they had ever been apart. Marvin and Yonna called them every day and made sure they were available whenever anyone needed them, but it wasn't the same as them being right there. She missed her father's proud smile after she laughed at one of his corny jokes. She missed the voices her mother made when telling Jacob old folktales about tar-covered tricksters or gods of thunder and lightning. She missed seeing her parents together, the way they moved in a constant dance, always close but never in each other's way. And there they were, finally. Just feet away in the sloped driveway.

Marsha stood by the window on her tiptoes to see over all of the luggage. Her excitement almost made her overlook the car her parents drove. Almost. A 2008 black Cadillac CTS, her father's gift to himself on his most recent birthday. She remembered going with him to the dealership to pick it out. In between negotiations with the salesman, Marvin answered her endless questions about what horsepower was and why red cars got higher insurance rates, always lowering his voice before adding little tricks of the trade and predictions of how the next part of the deal would play out. In the end, she was just glad he got the model with the heated seats. The ride home was the first of only a few times she actually rode in the car. Usually she rode in the Tahoe because it could fit the whole family with Jacob's car seat. Her ball of excitement dropped into a nervous pit at the bottom of her stomach. Questions and possibilities started swelling in Marsha's head. How did they get the Cadillac down here? Where's all of the luggage gonna go? She started to feel sick, as if the excitement were a plague leeching its way into her bloodstream. Something was wrong.

The plague dispersed as soon as her parents finally entered the hazy sunlit room in the front of the house. Jacob came running in and latched onto their mother's hip before she could make it fully in the door. Marissa, Jeremy, and Aunt Marybell were close behind, all smiling and greeting each other. With the baby pinned to her hip, their mother hugged and kissed Marissa on the cheek and squeezed Aunt Marybell. Jeremy lifted his chest and stretched himself up, comparing his new height with his father's. After a proud nod of approval, Marvin gently pulled his son into a headlock and kissed the top of his head to remind him who the father was.

Letting the boy free, Marvin saw Marsha, still standing by the window. She was just gleaming, waiting to be noticed. Cramps crept up his jaw line as he hid his nerves from his face. Gently, he lifted his daughter's chin to see the brown in her eyes.

"So, baby girl, what happened in the next chapter of *The Obsidian*? Did Soleste find out who Jehoshaphat was?"

"I can't spoil this one, Daddy. You have to read it yourself," Marsha said, smiling from ear to ear. He smiled back and hugged her tight into his cheek, lifting her feet slightly off the ground. Marsha clung on to her father's neck, making her feel like she was Jacob's age again. The deep, sandalwood of his aftershave, the hum of his breath, her father's presence soothed each of her senses, devouring any negative thought left lingering in her mind.

It wasn't until they were about to sit down at the table for a late lunch that the plague of anxiety came back. It started when Aunt Marybell asked Jeremy, Marissa, and Marsha to put the food out on the table. There was broccoli salad, cornbread, barbeque chicken, and some leftover carrot cake with cream cheese icing. As she was going to pick up the cake, Marsha saw her mother and father talking to Aunt Marybell in the other room. Her mother's face looked grim and Aunt Marybell did nothing but shake her head, disappointment pulling the side of her mouth into a purse. Questions and probabilities surged throughout her body as she brought the cake into the dining room where Marissa was setting the table. Marissa looked up and immediately sensed the angst on her little sister's face.

"What's wrong?" Marissa asked, pausing from her task.

"Do you know where the Tahoe is?" Marsha said softly, still trying to hear the conversation the adults were having.

"It's not outside?"

"No, they drove Daddy's Cadillac."

"Hm, that's strange. Maybe they drove it to Key West. You know Daddy feels like he's the man whenever he drives that car," Marissa poked.

Marsha was unamused.

"Well, how are we all gonna fit in there with the luggage?"

"I don't know Marsh, but I'm sure they'll tell us soon."

Marissa rubbed Marsha's arm gently. "You know what Mom always says, don't worry until you have something to worry about."

But as badly as she wanted to trust Marissa's advice, Marsha did have something to worry about. Their mother also always stressed the importance of trusting their instincts. Still, Marissa had a point. Whatever was going on, she'd find out soon enough.

Aunt Marybell emerged from the room with a hand on her hip and called everyone to the table. Once seated, they all joined hands and closed their eyes in prayer.

"Almighty God," Marvin began, "we thank you for the multitude of blessings this day has brought forth. We thank you for your protection during our travels, and for the wonderful reunion with our children and family. We ask that you bless the hands that prepared this food, and witness our gratitude as we receive this nourishment."

"Amen," the children chimed at the familiar prayer, but Marvin continued.

"We also ask for your guidance as we navigate the complexities of our lives and keep the importance of family at the forefront of our minds. Amen."

"Amen," Aunt Marybell enunciated with a twang that felt like a backhanded compliment.

Marsha peeked at the faces around the table while they passed the dishes around. Had no one else caught the revised ending to the prayer? Aunt Marybell's attitude? Was Marsha the only one strung enough to care?

As soon as everyone had food on their plate and had taken a few bites, her father cleared his throat and announced, "Your mother and I have some things to share with you."

Marsha knew this was it. Whatever he was about to say would explain the Cadillac, the talk with Aunt Marybell, the prayer ... all of it.

"Did you bring us something back?" Jeremy blurted, unconcerned.

"Something like that," their father said in a tone Marsha didn't recognize coming from his mouth. Was it nervousness? No way. Their father didn't get nervous, and yet, she could almost make out a shake in his voice. He took another pause to wipe his mouth with the napkin Marissa set out with his place setting. Or was it to buy him more time?

"A few weeks ago," he began, "right after we got to Key West, we got a call from your Uncle Tre."

The mood in the room shifted. Uncle Tre was like a myth in the family. The children knew he existed, but he was never really spoken of. Marsha knew her father and his twin had some serious issues but she didn't know what exactly happened. As a matter of fact, she had never really put much thought into it until now.

"My brother is very sick," Marvin said frankly.

"Uncle Tre's belly still hurts?" Jacob asked in his sweet, innocent voice, trying to make sense of his father's words.

"Yes, baby, Uncle Tre's belly is hurting real bad," their mother soothed. "We came back as quickly as we could and went to see how he was doing."

"Is he alive?" Jeremy obnoxiously interrupted before Marvin could continue.

Their father shot him a stern, disapproving look.

"He is," Marvin replied sharply, picking up where he was cut off. "But there are some things we need to do to help make sure he stays that way. So, we have actually been here for the past few weeks trying to figure some things out and ..."

"Here, as in Ocala?" Marsha interrupted, "And you didn't come get us?"

"Excuse you," her mother corrected. "Your father is still speaking."

Marsha lowered her head, somewhat surprised by her mistake. Jeremy had just gotten *the look* for doing the same exact thing. She didn't mean to be rude, the anxiety was simply eating her alive.

"Listen, I know you all will have a lot of questions. But let me finish and some of them might get answered."

Marvin turned to Marsha.

"Yes, baby, we've been here in Ocala for a little more than three weeks. We had a lot to do because, well ... we're not going back to Maryland. We've moved here."

Marsha didn't hear much after that. The plague exploded in her stomach and took over every cell of her body. It tried to rewrite her truth using the few words that penetrated its suffocating boundary. Words like "cancer," "grandpa's land," and "new school." They circled in her head until reality finally set in. Marsha couldn't take it. She stood up from the table, silencing the rapidly intensifying conversation, and walked away without looking back.

By the time Marsha got to her room, her face was soaked with tears. *Moved? To Ocala?* It was a nightmare too horrific to have imagined. Maryland was the only home she had ever known. What about her friends? Her track team? The lady that lived at the end of the street who gave out gallon Ziploc bags of candy for Halloween? She didn't know what hurt more, the fact that she didn't even get the chance to say goodbye, or the fact that her parents had known for weeks and didn't say a word. Marsha buried her face into the pillow on the bed she had shared with Marissa all summer and sobbed until the pillowcase stuck to her face. She had no idea how much time had passed when she heard a soft knock on the door.

"Please leave me alone," she pleaded. Marsha didn't want to talk. She didn't want to listen. She didn't want to do anything but cry.

III

The door squeaked open and a warm hand came to rest on her back.

"Marsh," a voice said softly. Marsha looked up through blurry, tear-filled eyes to find Marissa, perhaps the only person in the world that Marsha could bear to see. Marissa sat on the bed and without words, pulled her little sister in close and held her tight.

Time slipped away for a while until Marsha finally lifted her head, ready to address reality again. Her eyes felt no better than when they were stung red by the pool's chlorine.

"You okay?" Marissa asked her, still gently tracing her fingers through the pattern woven into Marsha's hair.

"Yeah," Marsha said softly. "Just a headache."

Marissa leaned over to meet Marsha's eyes. "Let's take these cornrows out, that will help a little."

Marsha rolled to her side on her sister's lap, where Marissa could reach the tips of her hair, and let the careful scratch of her sister's nails soothe her. Marsha sat wrapped in the warmth of the wordless gesture of care until it was time to leave for their new home.

PART II
CALLED

IV

MARSHA'S NEW ROOM FELT STERILE, LIKE A ROOM in the ICU of a hospital. The walls were painted a light gray with no pictures or decorations hanging on them, just some essentials sitting in the corners of the small room—a plastic dresser with a few partially filled drawers, her open suitcase, and a mattress without a bedframe. It rested by the open window in the back corner, where Marsha had fallen asleep under her sheets reading with her flashlight. Suddenly, she was startled awake by a rustling sound. Her eyes opened wide under her cocooned covers, and she carefully watched the shadows on her wall made by the fallen flashlight. She listened, hoping it was just the wind.

Another rustle. It was getting closer, whatever it was.

Is it a squirrel? A raccoon? Do they even have raccoons in Florida? Is it an alligator? Are alligators the raccoons of Florida? Focus Marsha ... May-

be it's that man you always see sitting at the computer in the library. Maybe he followed you home to kidnap you and sell you for a trip to Maui!

Marsha peeked her head from under the covers and scanned the floor for a weapon.

Her toiletry bag was open and falling out of her suitcase about an arm's length away. The long metal bottom of a comb rested softly on the carpet.

I can do some damage with a rattail ... at least enough to get away ...

She grabbed the comb and there was another rustle, this time longer, louder ...

WHOOOSH!!!

Suddenly a large bird flew through the window and perched itself right on top of the suitcase. In one motion, Marsha grabbed the comb and sat straight up on her bed, the pointed end ready to attack. She hated birds, but she was entirely too shocked to scream. The intruder did nothing, and the two stared at each other for a moment before it jerked its head to the side, as if to ask, "Am I really that threatening?"

The bird hopped down onto the floor just feet from Marsha, who flinched, clenching the comb tighter. Unmoved, the bird hopped closer until it stopped just before her, bringing with it the calm realization that this could just be a dream. Dreaming was nothing new to Marsha, it happened often and vividly, just like it did for her father. One of her favorite things to do with him was try to interpret the cryptic adventures and symbols their dreams would present. He always attempted to give a rational explanation for the strange happenings in the dream world, explaining that "dreams reflect what the subconscious dwells on." Her heart sank at the thought of him and everything that had occurred that day.

By the time they reached the new house, Marsha's sadness had evolved into anger, and instead of taking it out on any and everyone, she decided to read about something that she hated even more than her current reality. *Birds of Florida, a Field Guide* was a worthy selection from the stack of boxes sitting in the front room. Lowering the comb slowly, Marsha glanced down at the book she had fallen asleep reading. She recognized the bird from her studies. It was a common mockingbird, Mimus Polyglottos. It was small with a dark gray beak, white chest, and gray body. Its feathers were tipped with black and outlined with a thin, white strip. Coincidentally, it also happened to be the state bird of Florida. The mockingbird flew to the windowsill and looked back at Marsha, waiting for her to follow. Marsha ignored it and laid back down.

No way I'm following some bird out into the Florida wilderness in the middle of the night. With their alligator raccoons?! Uh-uh-uh. Not I. Marsha Claire Swallowtail will not end up on an Animal Planet special.

The mockingbird flew back to the floor of her room. "Come!" it chirped, startling Marsha. She heard the chirp, but she also heard a voice. It was a man's voice—raspy, muffled, and echoey.

Well that's a new development ... talking animals?

Just as Marsha was about to protest, "COME!" the mockingbird chirped again, with an intensified reverberation in its tone.

It flew back to the window and peered back at her once more.

"Quickly! Not much time!"

And out the window it went.

Okay, snap out of it. This is YOUR dream. YOU are in control.

She repeated the line her father had taught her a few times before she was interrupted once more.

"Quickly!" the mockingbird squawked from the darkness.

Something about the talking bird intrigued Marsha, and in that moment she decided, against her better judgment, that she would go. What could happen to her that was worse than what already happened earlier that day? Keeping hold of the comb, she threw her legs over her bed and into her slippers, then climbed out of the first-story window into the thickness of the humid Florida night.

The mockingbird was sitting on the loquat tree planted on the side of the house.

"This way!" it squawked, taking off. Marsha followed it along, tip-toeing down the side of her new house into the unfamiliar terrain of their backyard.

Marsha stopped at the edge of the tree line.

"I'm not going in there!" she whispered loudly, hugging her elbows around the pajamas she made from her father's old FSU T-shirt and plaid cotton pants. The mockingbird reappeared and hovered in the air right before her.

"I'm not going in there. There's probably an alligator waiting for me right when I step into that bush!"

"Your dream. You in control," the bird echoed before flying out of sight once more.

Marsha conceded. How did the bird know about her and her father's saying? The strangeness of the dream drew Marsha in like the sharp breath she took before struggling through the bush after the bird.

The pair continued this way through the moonlit night. Moving from tree to tree and post to post, the mockingbird led Marsha to an open field of dogfennel. There were blueberries and blackberries bordering the circular forest line of the clearing. In the center stood a massive southern live oak tree, posing majestically above the brush. The tree stretched wildly in every direction. Its branches winded and warped like a dance to the wisp of hurricane winds. The newest twigs reached high enough to kiss the moon. The oldest, thick with years, fell low enough to hug the ground. The bird flew off ahead of Marsha and disappeared into the tree's shadows. A short moment later a man appeared, tall and shadowy, emerging from behind the tree's thick trunk.

"Whew, I'm glad you came, Marsha. I can't lie, I wasn't sure if you'd make it out that window."

She knew that voice, but it couldn't be. She hadn't heard that voice in years.

The figure stepped out of the shadow and Marsha lit up like the full moon above them.

"Uncle VanDyke!"

Marsha ran to embrace her great-uncle and was shocked by his strength as he picked her up and twirled her around.

"You're walking! You're TALKING!"

"I sure am!" Uncle VanDyke laughed. "Ohhhhh, it's just so good to see you! How ya doing lil' girl?"

"It's so good to *hear you*!" Marsha said, a smile wide across her face. Her uncle had lost his ability to speak after a stroke when Marsha was still in elementary school. With it went his ability to crack the perfect joke in the wrong moment, spin fantastic stories from his teenage years, and, most heartbreakingly, make his trumpet sound like a hundred harmonizing hums. He had survived, but only in the way his trumpet had—a corroded brass frame without the breath to blow a tune. Aunt Marybell and Uncle VanDyke played the role of grandparents so well, Marsha rarely thought of her true grandparents who died when she was an infant. The stroke was the first time Marsha truly dealt with the loss of a family member, and memories of that time still left a lump in her throat.

"You wouldn't believe what is happening right now," Marsha started, nearly stuttering over her words at the chance to vent to the uncle she missed so much. "We've been staying with you guys all summer while Mommy and Daddy were supposed to be on vacation.

"Well. They. Weren't. They were actually going behind our backs to move all of our things to Ocala. They bought a whole new house right down the street from you and Aunt Marybell's! WITHOUT TELLING US! They tried to make excuses for it, saying Uncle Tre needs help and something about some land, but I couldn't get past the fact that they LIED!"

Marsha's heart was beating faster with each word. If it weren't for the excitement and joy she felt from seeing her uncle, the anger would have taken over.

"So, fast forward to earlier when I fell asleep in this strange bedroom in this strange house—can you believe I woke up to a mockingbird trying to attack me! Or, at least that's what I thought at first. Instead, it started talking! That's even crazier, right? So I figured it had to be a dream! I ended up following it and it led me here where I found you!"

"Yeah, sorry about that. I know you don't like birds too much," Uncle VanDyke chuckled, bringing Marsha's rant to a screeching stop.

She thought back to what he said when he first appeared from behind the tree: "I wasn't sure if you'd make it out that window."

Uncle VanDyke smirked while he watched Marsha struggle to put the pieces together. "That's right, the mockingbird was me. It's easier to travel like that in the Traverse."

Marsha shook her head in confusion.

"The Traverse? I ... I don't ..."

"I know, I know. It doesn't make much sense. That's how I felt when I first got here too. But I'm afraid we don't have time for too much of an explanation," Uncle VanDyke said compassionately. "What I can tell you is this. What you said earlier, about this being a dream, it is in some ways, but it's more like a space in between the dream world and the spirit world. One with its own consciousness and one that is constantly changing. I wouldn't go as far as to say you're in control, but it does respond to the things you ask for."

"Okay ... so what about the whole bird thing? Is that something you asked for?"

"No, not quite. I actually don't really know how that happened, but it is pretty cool, right?"

He spun around into a blurred ball of gray and white before her eyes, emerging as a mockingbird, then spinning again and turning back into Uncle VanDyke.

"HOW?!" Marsha marveled, spinning around to try to make the magic work herself.

"When I find out, I'll tell you. How about that?" Uncle VanDyke resolved.

"Deal," Marsha said, still giddy and full from his company. "So if this isn't a dream, why did you bring me here?" Marsha asked.

"Now that is the question of the hour. There is something important I gotta show you." Uncle VanDyke motioned for Marsha to follow him closer to the large oak tree.

"Like I said, the Traverse is in between the spirit realm and the dream world. Spirits exist here and so do dreams, but not like they do in their own separate realms. In the Traverse, spirits can only exist as animals, and people can usually come in their dreams."

"So is that what you're doing when I see you in the real world? Dreaming?"

"Honestly, Marsha. I haven't quite figured that out yet. But in the time that I have spent here, I have learned a lot about spirits and how to talk with them. Most of them stick to themselves because their descendants would rather not interact with them as directly as they could. It's a scary thing, you see, to talk to ghosts. But people like me, and I guess people like you, can learn to speak to us and vice versa. I live in a different tree closer to my Mary, but this tree right here along with all of the birds in it, well this tree is yours."

"Mine?"

"Yep, all of you! Jacob, Marissa, Jeremy, and your father, too. This is the Swallowtail family tree."

At that moment, the tree erupted with life. Dozens of large white and black raptor-like birds flooded the outer edges of the branches as if they had been waiting for the perfect moment to reveal themselves. They had large white chests and black wings and tails, and were singing and squawking as they went about their business without looking at Marsha.

Marsha's face fell. Of course they were all birds, and not only birds, but *these* birds.

"Swallow-tailed kites," she said, halfway to herself. "You can tell by the shape of their tails and that stupid high-pitched song they sing. Why couldn't they be butterflies?" She rolled her eyes at the tree, but something about it held her gaze.

"Hey now, these are your ancestors. Your people. Your family. You might not understand what that means yet but showing them respect is not an option." Uncle VanDyke looked down at her with one critical eyebrow raised. "Where's that attitude coming from anyway? That's not the Marsha I know."

"It's been a long summer, Uncle VanDyke. And I hear you when you say they are my family, but ..." Marsha finally tore her eyes from the tree. "I don't know them. To me, my family is and has always been my parents, my siblings, Aunt Marybell, and you. Plus, I hate birds."

"Now I do remember that," he laughed. "Do you remember that time those cranes were in the backyard and—"

"Yes," Marsha interrupted, "no one lets me forget it."

The summer before Uncle VanDyke's stroke, while the family was on a road trip to Disney World, they stopped in Ocala for a visit. Marsha, maybe seven or eight years old, was playing outside with Jeremy when two sandhill cranes silently landed in the back of the lot. Jeremy saw them and let them get real close before telling Marsha to turn around. When she did, the cranes were towering over her, and scared her so bad she wet her pants. Everyone thought it was a hilarious story considering how gentle the cranes can be, but not Marsha. She'd hated all birds ever since.

"You sure know a lot about the birds you claim to hate ..."

"You gotta know your enemy, Uncle VanDyke."

He chuckled, "Well, alright now."

Marsha returned her attention to the tree and the busy birds bustling about in its branches.

The more she studied, the more she could see the details that set each bird apart. One had very bushy chest feathers. Another had a bluish tint to the black of its wing. Another's tail feathers were more distinctly sharp at the corners. She felt a swell of emotion building in her throat. She knew she had more family, but her grandparents were gone and her uncle was just a whisper whose name came and passed like a rare breeze. She didn't even have any fake cousins from aunties and uncles that were really just close friends of the family. Until now, the family she knew had always been enough. The sight of the tree and all of the lives she was supposably connected to sparked a longing in her, a loneliness that felt like a child too small to reach their mother's neck for a snuggle. The comfort was so close and still just out of reach.

"Ancestors? So like, all of my great-great-great-grandparents, aunts and uncles, and stuff?"

"That's right," her uncle said patiently, letting her take it all in. "Not all of them though. You have many, many more. These are just the ones that flew back."

Marsha's questions and emotions overflowed like a levee during a flood, and the levee was breaking.

"Flew back? Flew back from where? And why? Why did they all choose *this* tree? And what about the ones who didn't? Why can't they hear me talking like you can? How do you know all of this? Why is this all happening now?"

"Woah woah woah, I know this is a lot, but all in due time, baby girl. Right now, we gotta get down to business. I can answer your last question. As a matter of fact, that's why we've brought you here."

Marsha followed him around the trunk of the tremendous tree as he continued explaining.

"I have been sitting under this tree for God knows how long trying to get someone to come see this. I've sent for my Mary, your siblings, and even your father, who I thought for sure would come. He was always dreaming as a little boy." Uncle VanDyke shrugged. "But no one did. No one until you."

Marsha started to question why she herself came. Why did she get out of her bed in the middle of the night to follow a talking bird, of all things, into this strange bushy clearing? But the biggest question still remained.

"Come for what? Why am I here Uncle VanDyke?!" Marsha tried

hard not to let her impatience come off as disrespectful. The old man took a few more steps around the tree and pointed up.

"For that."

On the back side of the tree, the whole setting changed. The branches were barren. The leaves had fallen, and there were no birds bustling about. Uncle VanDyke pointed at one of the larger branches where a small fire burned slowly, but constantly. Marsha's jaw fell open and her eyes widened in fear.

"What are you waiting for! We have to put it out!" In a panic, she searched around for any sign of water, but Uncle VanDyke took hold of her shoulders and turned her to face him. He squatted low enough to look her straight in the eyes.

"I need you to listen here, and listen close. This ain't the type of fire you can put out with water. I've tried that. A few weeks ago, I noticed the branch was burning, and it's been spreading further up ever since. Now, I don't know too much about what's going on in the real world. It's only when my body out there snaps back to life for a second or two that I can hear a little something, and even then it's so muffled and echoey that I can barely make it out. But what I hear from you, plus what I've seen here myself, I know something has to be going on that's much bigger than what it all seems."

Marsha lowered her eyes in guilt. Maybe if she'd listened a little longer at lunch, or let her mother talk to her when she tried earlier that evening, she'd have some information that could help. Still, the thought of speaking to her parents made Marsha's stomach churn.

"Listen, we don't have time for you to tell me the full story right now 'cause you gotta get back to bed. But what you need to know is this. I can bet you that whatever is causing this tree to burn is what's causing your family to burn too. Nothing in the Traverse happens by chance. Since you're the only one who made it here, I bet you're the only one who can fix it. And if it has something to do with your family tree, then well ... I know Ocala is the last place you want to be, but it might be the one place you *need* to be."

Uncle VanDyke walked Marsha back towards her window while his words echoed in her ears and clouded her mind with questions and confusion. No matter what, Marsha had declared to herself, her first step once on the other side of this dream would be finding out more about this strange world.

"How exactly did we get to the Traverse, Uncle VanDyke?"

"Well, that depends. You got here through your ability to dream. You've probably been here many times before, you just didn't know it. Was there a place you would go in your dreams in Maryland? Where it seemed like no matter what dream you were having, if it got too intense, you found yourself there?"

Marsha nodded. "Yes! It was the gazebo in the back of my neighborhood!"

Uncle VanDyke smiled and slowly nodded his head then continued, "As for me, I'm not really sure how I got here. Last thing I remember was losing feeling on my side, and your Aunt Marybell calling for help. When I woke up, I was here. I lived an interesting and eventful life, Marsha. My Mary and I had a ball. But that all came with a price, and sometimes, it costs you more than what's on the price tag. But listen lil' girl, this is all a story for another time. You have enough on your plate already with putting this fire out. Plus, there goes your window right there."

Marsha looked up at the foreign window left open and bare without blinds to block the dim glow of the flashlight. She wasn't ready to say goodbye to Uncle VanDyke, especially with the questions twisting her thoughts.

"Okay now, Marsha. Now that you know you're in the Traverse, I can't tell you how to get back, and I can't promise I'll be here when you do. You'll be fine though, you're a pro. Still, be careful. I'm not gonna tell you not to wander. I'm just gonna say this: things aren't always exactly as they seem here. Stuff can get real strange, and if anything gets out of hand, remember what I told you earlier. The Traverse does respond to the things you ask for. Try that little saying your daddy taught you. It should do just fine."

Marsha nodded, and considered her uncle's words closely. Then she gave him a hug, and climbed into the window, stopping to look at the tree once more. Marsha could see the faint glow of fire, but what she couldn't see was smoke. There was no smoke.

How am I supposed to know how to put a fire like that out?

Marsha hoped that this was like all of the other dreams she'd had in the past, where she woke up and continued her life essentially unaffected. She knew, deep down inside, however, that it wasn't. And either way, when she woke up the next day, everything in her life would be different.

Two weeks passed without Marsha waking up in the Traverse, and the momentum of her new life in Ocala eventually swept away the memory of the dream. Her first day of school was just a day away and Marsha still hadn't told her friends back home in Maryland that she had moved. When the group chat buzzed with summer stories, new schedules, and debates over what table they would sit at during third lunch, Marsha ignored them. But of course it was Abby who asked if she was back from Florida yet. Although all four girls grew up together, Abby stuck with Marsha, and Marsha with Abby. They were a surprising duo—where Marsha was quiet and critical, Abby was forthright and outgoing. She always made sure Marsha was part of the conversation, whether or not Marsha wanted to be. Abby made Marsha feel seen.

Telling Abby meant that every part of the move was real, and she wasn't ready for that.

"Not yet. Still here)': " she texted back.

A slew of texts came in after her response.

"marshaaaaaaaa!!!" - Breonna K.

"how's florida???" - Breonna K.

"any cute boys <3?" - Breonna K.

"Hey marsh! when r u coming back? wat's ur schedule? do u have 2nd or 3rd lunch?" - Chels

"Ur n honors rite?????" - Breonna K.

"Duhhhh. Ur super smart :P" - Breonna K.

"U prolly hav 3rd lunch wit us!!!!!!"

"Girl I was wondering where you been. I MISS YOU! <3! Can't wait to see you!!" - Abby

Marsha rolled her eyes. First of all, Marissa was the only person who could call her Marsh, but Chelsea Hernandez always ignored her, saying the A made Marsha too long. Second, why did Breonna use so much punctuation? It always felt like she was yelling at you, wide-eyed and frantic.

Opening up a new message, Marsha texted Abby alone.

"hey, can i call u tonight?"

"of course! cant wait" - Abby

Anger settled over Marsha as she realized she might not ever see Abby again. But she was tired of feeling angry, and decided that a bowl of cereal and a good book would do the trick.

Her days were busy enough as it was. Jeremy and Marissa spent most of their time practicing at their new high school to prepare for fall sports tryouts, so Marsha was left with her parents to help out with, well, everything. Entertaining Jacob, putting together Ikea pieces, shopping. There was so much shopping. Furniture shopping. Decoration shopping. School supply shopping. There wasn't one day that their mother didn't haul Marsha and Jacob in and out of at least five stores as she and Marvin tried to make Ocala their home again as quickly as they could.

Marsha couldn't lie, she liked what her mother had done to the place. The new house was a neighborhood over from Aunt Marybell's, but the houses on Marsha's street were a newer build and slightly bigger. Even though she and her siblings still shared one bathroom, at least there was a small extra one off of the kitchen for emergencies. Plus, Marsha's room had a walk-in closet. Like every house in the neighborhood, there was a screened-in pool in the backyard, but no basement to escape to, something that only reminded Marsha how different Ocala was than Accokeek.

Marsha heard her mother approaching the front room, where she had claimed a spot under the large bay window looking out onto the front lawn. They crafted it into a sitting room doubling as a library, a decision that Marsha wondered if she had influenced. She was reading the final book from her new school's summer reading list, which she had crushed over the past few weeks.

"*Bronze Star.* I've heard of Shannon Dexter, but don't think I've read this one," her mother said softly as she sat on the floor next to her daughter. "How do you like it so far?"

"Mm, it's okay. I like the way she writes. She makes it seem like I'm there. And I really like Amari, the main character."

"So what makes it just *okay*?"

Without looking up, Marsha thought for a moment while finishing the page. She was about a quarter way through the book she had started earlier that morning.

"It's just that, why do all stories about black people have to be about slavery and hard times, or overcoming something terrible in order to be the first to do something? What if I want to read about a ditsy, privileged black woman who daydreams about a mysterious man and his green light across the bay. Or a black boy with a superhero complex who is responsible for learning and keeping all of the memories that make us human?"

"Because those aren't our stories, baby."

"So our stories are of hardship. That's it?"

"Of course not."

Marsha looked up at her mother while Yonna searched for words.

"When I was very little, my grandmother would tell me stories from Ayiti about great warriors who guarded and protected their people, and good witches who could turn the day to night, and back again. Stories about a foolish Uncle Bouki and tricky Ti Malice."

Yonna didn't talk about her childhood much. She was born in Haiti, and her mother abandoned her, leaving her with her grandmother when she was just an infant. The two migrated to Florida before Yonna could even walk. When the old lady died, seven-year-old Yonna was left in the hands of the state. For about a year, she bounced around from group home to foster home until a couple of young doctors adopted her and another older girl. She never got to know this girl very well because as soon as she turned eighteen, she left the family and was never heard from again. After that, the family moved to Ocala where Yonna grew up an only child.

"I never forgot those stories," Yonna continued, "or how they made me laugh, made me scared, or made me feel like having Ayiti in my blood meant I was somebody. I belonged somewhere. I carry them with me everywhere I go. I always have."

"Yeah, I used to love those stories!" Marsha reflected.

"I can tell you one later ... if that's not too childish for you," Yonna said, gently digging her shoulder into Marsha's arm.

"Mommm," Marsha giggled, trying to brush her off. "I'll ... get back to you."

"The stories I read about black people don't make me feel like your stories made you feel. I feel tired. And angry sometimes. But mostly tired." She shook her head, her coiled hair bouncing as she processed her fatigue. "It's hard to want to read them, but it's hard to stop, too. I like learning about us, but I don't like feeling bad when I'm reading."

"You know baby, a lot of our best stories are told by mouth, just like the ones my grandmother told. She didn't have any books, just memories and experiences."

Yonna got up abruptly, then took her daughter's hands to pull her up as well.

"I just happen to know the best place in Ocala to get some stories. I gotta make a phone call. Go throw on some clothes and meet me down here in fifteen minutes."

When her mom revealed that they were going to the hair salon, Marsha felt truly excited for the first time since the news of the move. She hadn't even thought about getting her hair done for school and the realization brought about bittersweet feelings. Still, she missed her mother, and even though she was still mad at her parents, she appreciated the quality time she'd be able to spend while getting her hair braided.

They pulled into the small parking lot of an aged adobe building with three small storefronts. The far one was a barbershop, in the middle was a juice bar, and on the end was Loretta's Beauty Salon. Marsha looked up at her mother who wore a nostalgic smile on her face.

"You know baby, I've been coming here since I was a little girl, younger than you."

"Really?"

"Uh huh, and I'll tell you what, I always left with more than just a new hairdo."

A swell of voices and rich scents of bergamot and castor oil hugged Marsha as they approached the door of the salon. When they entered, the little bell at the top of the door jingled softly under the conversation, which seemed to be at its peak. The ladies inside carried on as if they didn't even notice, hooting and hollering, with each voice competing for dominance.

In the front of the shop was a small reception desk with several chairs placed on either side of the door. Sitting on the coffee table to the right were several magazines with beautiful black women on the covers. A woman flipped through a braid edition, each style woven crisply into intricate designs. On the left, another woman sat next to a large display shelf holding beautifully handcrafted earrings, necklaces, and bangle sets, hair products with little black girls on the packaging, and a few different colors of braiding hair.

Further into the shop, there were six large chairs, three on either side of the room. Behind the chairs along the walls were huge mirrors with lights all around them, and a countertop that held up countless supplies and instruments. Although each station was set up the same way, they were all unique in their organization and decor. One of the mirrors was decorated with fake yellow and white flowers, and Marsha hoped that would be where she sat. There were drawers and cubbies, some closed and some bursting open with beads and hair accessories. At every station, there were large spherical glasses filled with the same blue liquid holding several rattail combs and small brushes with the ends sticking out. She had never seen so many hot combs and curling irons in her life. All but two chairs were occupied. The woman who seemed to have won the battle of the voices was almost done getting her hair braided into long, silver plaits while pointing at the TV screen.

"See! See! I told you! I told you! That girl gon' have to pay that man some money!"

In the back of the shop, there were two large black sinks where one of the stylists was rinsing out her client's hair.

"What happened? What happened?" the lady said loudly over the rushing water.

"Ms. Monroe, I'ma need you to stay still. You my first client of the day and I'm not tryna end up all wet," said her stylist, a young woman maybe a few years older than Marissa. All of the skilled women, who could transform both hair and mood with their hands, wore thin black aprons over their clothes—except this stylist, who wore a thicker, protective smock on top.

To the left of the sinks was a door with a restroom sign and four chairs connected to large, hooded hair dryers. Two of those chairs were also occupied. One woman with a head full of curlers was minding her business, fiddling on her PalmPilot. The other lady, whose hair was in a wrap set, looked like she was about to jump out of her seat as her eyes stayed glued to the TV set mounted in the upper corner of the room.

"Girl, he brought out the photos. That man came with receipts!"

"I'll be right with you ma'am," the young stylist said over the sound of the rest of the ladies chiming in with their opinions.

Just then, the little bell jingled again as Marsha and her mother took a seat in the waiting area. A large old woman burst through the door carrying several bags of hair. Although she looked ancient, she moved as if she weren't a day over thirty-five. It seemed like every woman stopped mid-sentence to greet the famous Mrs. Loretta Warren.

"Hey, Lo!"

"How ya doin', Loretta?"

She greeted them back then turned to Marsha and her mother.

"Yonna Swallowtail, I thought I'd heard a ghost when I answered your phone call, as long as it's been since I've heard from you! Come give me a hug and help me with these bags."

Marsha watched her mom embrace the lady for a long moment, and as usual, took a moment to scan her surroundings, waiting to be seen. Yonna took the bags and walked them over to Mrs. Lo's station. Then the old lady turned to Marsha, as if sensing her anticipation.

"And you must be Marsha. I haven't seen you since you were a chunky little baby on your momma's hip. What a beautiful young lady you have grown into."

Mrs. Loretta's presence was warm and familiar, and Marsha couldn't help but smile from ear to ear. Plus, nobody had ever called her beautiful besides Marissa and her parents, and they were supposed to say things like that.

"I'm so glad you could fit us in! I know it was such short notice," Yonna said walking back to the front.

"Now Yonna, I would clear my schedule for you anytime. What's funny is, today's client canceled just ten minutes before you called. So, whose head is it that I'm doing today?" The woman looked at Marsha as if she knew the answer to her own question.

"You know I don't do braids in the summer, Mrs. Loretta. It's too hot for all that. But Marsha here is starting seventh grade tomorrow over at Silver Springs Middle, so we gotta get her right."

"Well alright now, let's get this show on the road. I wanna get as much done as I can before it gets too hot and my fingers start to swell up. Follow me, Miss Marsha Claire Swallowtail. And Yonna, you might as well grab that chair and come over too. Sounds like you got a lot to catch me up on."

"She knows my middle name?" Marsha whispered as her mother collected her things from the chair.

"Yeah baby, Mrs. Loretta knows just about everything."

Marsha picked up some bags of hair and followed the woman over to the booth with the white flowers.

"Okay baby, you see that woman over there?" Mrs. Loretta pointed at the young woman by the wash station. "That's my granddaughter, Kimberly, but you can call her Bee. She's gonna get you washed up then send you back over to me when it's time. Go'on now."

"I have a special smock for you, pretty girl," Bee said warmly as she reached into a deep basket next to the sink. She pulled out a smock with the same white flowers that decorated Mrs. Loretta's station. She wrapped a hand towel around her neck then fastened the smock tight over Marsha's clothes in a dramatic gesture. Marsha was starting to feel overwhelmed with how nice everyone was, but she made sure not to show it.

"I know y'all don't have this nonsense playing in my shop," Marsha heard Mrs. Loretta say over the warm rushing water.

"C'mon Lo, you know this is the only place I can come to watch my shows ever since my daughter moved me into her house. I'm just about done anyway, ain't that right Lauren?"

"Yeah, Mrs. Loretta, I only have about four braids left."

"Four braids is liable to take you 'bout forty-five minutes."

"Now you know you wrong for that, Bee."

The whole shop erupted in laughter and Marsha giggled a bit under the scrubs. The hair salon she went to in Maryland was nice, and her stylist always did a great job, but Mrs. Loretta knew her middle name.

She could see why her mother had been coming for so long. As much as she wanted to hate Ocala, Mrs. Loretta didn't necessarily make her want to leave.

After Marsha's hair was washed and blow-dried, Mrs. Loretta started parting it into sections to be braided. She asked Marsha if she wanted it all one color, or if she wanted a few highlights throughout. With her mother's permission, she chose to get the highlights. By then, the show was off and the ladies were all talking to one another about the new roads being built and how there oughta be more crossing guards this year around the elementary school. There was a debate about an old liquor store that closed down, and another about the remodeling of a local shopping center. All the ladies, however, could agree on the fact that more black folk needed to invest in businesses, and aim to own the buildings they were in, like Mrs. Loretta and the other shop owners in the small plaza. The lady with the silver braids was named Steffany Clarke, but everyone called her Ne. It was her daughter who owned the juice spot next door, and a man named Wallace owned the barber shop. All three owners not only ran their businesses, but owned the land they operated on.

A couple hours passed and the shop began to clear out. Some of the stylists went to get lunch together and Ms. Ne still sat in the same chair flipping through one of the magazines. Bee had taken over for her grandmother and was working on the middle of Marsha's hair while Yonna and Loretta spoke in the neighboring chair. She knew better than to make it known that she was listening in on grown folks talk, so she tried her best to keep her eyes pointed at the TV while her ears pointed at the conversation.

"So y'all are back for good, huh?"

"It's looking that way," Yonna said with a sigh.

"God is good 'cause I never would have thought I'd see the day. I don't know what happened, but it must have been serious to cause Marvin to steal y'all outta town like that in the first place."

"He didn't steal us, it was a mutual decision. But ..." Yonna pointed her eyes towards Marsha.

"Okay okay, I understand. So what brings y'all back now?"

"Well, for one, Tre's getting worse ..."

"Worse? In health or habit?"

"Seems like both right now."

"That poor man could never seem to figure it out. But I've known them for a long, long time. Their mother used to bring them here with her when I first opened this shop. I know they're twins and all, but I still can't imagine Marvin would move y'all all back here just for Tre."

"You're right, he sure wouldn't. You know about that land over by the forest on the north side of town?"

Loretta clapped her hands a loud slap, startling Marsha.

"I knew it! Ne! I told you they were here to get that land back!"

"You know about what's going on?"

"Child, please," Loretta shooed. "As soon as I saw it in the paper I thought of Mikey. You couldn't have a conversation with him without hearing about getting that deed."

That was true. Marvin's father wasn't the friendliest man, and he kept a tight circle. But every person in that circle had heard about the land. The big question had always been where the official deed was.

"Yeah, I heard all about that too," Ne cut in. "How Tre barged into the city council meeting sounding just like Mikey talking 'bout, 'That's Swallowtail land!'" Ne deepened her voice and tightened her face, mocking him.

Marsha remembered her father saying something about some land when he first broke the news, but she had tried her best not to think about that moment since then. Now, something deep within her urged her to listen closely.

Mrs. Loretta bounced a little in her chair, giggling.

"No he didn't."

"Girl, yes he did. Whatever the case, something he said got y'all that extension. Are y'all really planning on going up against the city?" Ne asked Yonna. By now, the whole shop was tuned in.

"I don't know what they're planning yet," Yonna admitted. "But we agreed that all things considered, it was time to come back."

For Marsha, hearing her mother talk about her role in the decision to move threatened to bring all of her emotions back, but she couldn't seem to be angry with Mrs. Loretta around.

"And you? How do you feel about this move, Marsha Claire?" asked Mrs. Loretta, catching Marsha off guard.

"I'm okay."

"Now Marsha, I know you don't know me too well, but I'm a hard person to get one over on. It's okay baby, you can tell me how you really feel."

She took a moment to answer.

"I ... just wish they would have told us sooner," she finally said softly.

"Well," Loretta said, leaning back in her chair, "have you talked to them about it?"

Marsha looked at her mother who was clearly uneased by the question. For a split second, Marsha wondered if and how Mrs. Loretta knew that she had become a master of avoidance to all things concerning her parents.

"No, I haven't."

"Well, I see that it still hurts you baby and I'm sorry about that. But a wound like that is slow to heal on its own." Without standing, Mrs. Loretta took a few small steps to roll the wheeled chair closer to Marsha. "Before I moved here, I was just a young girl from Atlanta, waiting for my life to start. Then one day I fell in love with a soldier just getting back from Vietnam, and he said he wanted to bring me back home with him—back to Ocala, Florida. I had never heard of the place, but wherever he was going, I wanted to be, even if it meant I had to leave my family, my friends. Atlanta is a big city, but a small town. I grew up with those people. Still, I said, "Let's do it. Let's make it an adventure."

"And was it? Has it been an adventure?" Marsha asked, almost cutting the woman off. "Excuse me, I'm sorry."

Mrs. Loretta waved the apology off, then tensed her face in a moment of thought.

"You know, it has. But not in any way that I woulda expected back then. As much as I wanted it to be an adventure, I hated this place when I got here. It was country, and slow." Mrs. Loretta dragged the words out in an exaggerated southern accent. "And so quiet, it used to scare me sometimes.

"But then, something clicked. Nothing changed about Ocala, or how the town cared for me, I just finally embraced it. I started talking to people and going to different community events. Eventually I started doing hair and after that, the whole town felt like a warm hug, and it became an extension of my own family. Soon my folks in Atlanta started to come down and join the party. It was like one day I looked around and saw nothing but good people, honest people, like your grandfather. Mikey and Warner—my husband—they were best friends."

Marsha glanced at her mother in question. Her grandfather was someone else she didn't really know much about. Yonna smiled back and shrugged, then nodded her head towards Mrs. Loretta. Mrs. Loretta went on telling tales about Grandpa Mikey, Mr. Warner, and all of the trouble they started *and* solved during their time together on Earth. They were smart, hard-working, community-oriented men. Together, they owned the construction company that built the plaza, and made it a point that anyone who wanted to bring their business into a storefront would sign a rent-to-own contract. There were seven other plazas like this scattered throughout central Florida, home to over twenty businesses, all owned and operated by local black entrepreneurs. The more she learned, the more she began to see her father reflected in the words. His career in construction, and constant emphasis on community, education, and ownership—it was no accident who her father had become. Marsha could see it built into him like the walls of Mrs. Loretta's salon. Somehow, this eased the knot of anger in her chest. She trusted her parents, and if they decided that Ocala was what was best for everyone, maybe she could try to understand.

"The Swallowtail family has been in Ocala for a long long time, you understand me?" Mrs. Loretta continued, just as Bee dipped the tips of Marsha's braids into hot water. "Since your great-great-great-grand-mother, I believe. Even if it's hard for you to like it here, child, this is your home. Your blood runs through these streets just like it runs through your veins. You have people here. People like me. And others who will stand behind you simply because of your name. I know you aren't used to being around that kind of thing, but I get the sense that you, my dear, are wiser than your age suggests. That kind of love, that kind of support, it works in magical ways. It heals things."

Mrs. Loretta's words unlocked something inside of Marsha the same way staring up into her family tree did. She thought of all of the birds she saw with all of their differences and similarities. She wondered how many

V

people in this town she was connected to through them. Marsha looked at her mother who had never known her real family, and wondered how hard it was to leave the place and people who had filled that void.

"See, you know what I'm talking about," Mrs. Loretta continued, as if reading Marsha's mind. "If you let it, if you can get past the slow pace and new faces, Ocala will open its arms to you, just like it did for me."

VI

"YOU GETTING BIG BOY, I DON'T KNOW HOW much longer I can keep messin' around with you," Marvin panted, leaning over his knees, watching the giggling toddler standing on the couch.

"That's all you got?" Jacob's squeaky voice rebounded. The toddler's words still stumbled out of his mouth and Marvin couldn't help but chuckle. While Marvin worked to repair the rift between him and his older children, there was nothing he enjoyed more than escaping to spend time with the baby. Since Jacob didn't fully grasp everything that was going on, he was a source of light for Marvin as he navigated through his self-constructed tunnel of darkness. Jacob grew so much in the few weeks that Marivn and Yonna were away and his personality was really starting to show itself. He was confident, loyal, and as silly as can be. Every moment Marvin spent with Jacob since their return brought pride and surprise.

Marvin straightened himself up, then sat into a sumo squat mirroring his youngest child. After three large stomps, the pair ritualistically grunted and the match began. Jacob launched off the couch towards his father who caught him, and cradling his head, playfully slammed him onto the floor. Everything Jacob lacked in size, he made up for in pure energy, and Marvin caught himself needing to try much more than expected in a delicate dance between force and restraint. Through the child's screaming laughter, Marvin heard Jeremy's heavy, cadenced steps bounding down the stairs.

Tha-domp, tha-domp, tha-domp.

He rounded the corner into the living room just as Jacob had gotten the better of Marvin's arm, almost ending in a faceplant.

"Damn Dad, Jacob got you like that?"

Marvin chuckled, more surprised by Jeremy's language than anything else. He looped his arm around Jacob's waist, easily overpowering him, and stood up straight with the toddler squirming gleefully on his hip.

"Since when did you start cussin' in the house?"

"Chill, I was joking. It's not like I was cussin' *at* you," Jeremy responded dismissively with his head buried in the pantry.

At first, Marvin was slightly amused by his son's audacity. It could have just been a joke. But this, whether Jeremy knew it or not, was a step further. He put Jacob down and peered at Jeremy. Jacob, noticing his father's change of energy, took a pause from the wrestle match. Just before Jeremy met his father's gaze, Yonna walked through the door, with Marsha and Marissa following close behind. Yonna placed a few bags on the counter and scooped Jacob up into her arms. Marissa, still sporting her volleyball practice gear, shouted hello and ran upstairs to hop in the shower. After greeting his mother and sister, with three Uncrustables in one hand and a bottle of water under his arm, Jeremy stampeded behind Marissa before Marvin could get out a word.

BOOM! BOOM! BOOM! BOOM! BOOM!

"Y'all quit running in my house!" their mother yelled. "I swear that boy grew a hundred pounds this summer." She greeted Marvin with a kiss then headed upstairs with Jacob on her hip, negotiating whether or not it was bath time. Aside from Jacob, none of them seemed to notice the potentially intense moment they interrupted, wrapping Marvin in disorientation.

"Hey Daddy, you okay?"

The sound of his daughter's voice pulled him back to himself, but as always, he played it off well. Marvin looked down at his third child, the crisp diamond-patterned parts at the base of long black and golden braids shining like a halo around her head.

"Hey, baby girl! Your hair looks beautiful."

"You like it?" Marsha spun around then struck a pose, hair spreading out in a swirl around her before resting on the frontside of her shoulder.

"I love it! You gon' kill it as the new girl!" Marsha's face fell as his words set in and Marvin immediately knew he chose the wrong ones.

"Yeah," she sighed deeply and fell back onto the couch. Surprised she didn't run off and continue her silent treatment, Marvin cautiously slid onto the couch beside her. This was the first conversation they'd had since he broke the news. He waited patiently for Marsha to continue, deciding it was better to let her lead.

"I still have to tell Abby. But I'm kinda dreading it. I feel bad about waiting this long. I just hope she doesn't get too mad."

"Well, let's think. What if she does?"

"Worst case, I never see her again and she just stays mad forever."

"Best case?"

"She understands. We still talk all the time. And we visit each other when school is out."

"And in your experience, which one is Miss Abigail Clarke, your friend of over five years, more inclined towards?"

"Well, she doesn't like liars and she's not shy about it. She got pretty upset at Chelsea and Breonna when they lied about their sleepover during spring break. But eventually she got over it. Plus, she loves Florida, especially Disney World." Marsha thought for a moment longer. "As my extensive experience suggests," she playfully articulated every syllable, then shifted to a more soft, solemn tone, "she'll be mad at first, and that will stink. But then she'll start to understand."

"There you go then," Marvin said. "Evidence suggests a survivable situation." Marvin stretched his arm around his daughter, pressing out the distance his own lies created between them. As if he could feel the frays of their relationship binding together once more, one by one, gaining strength, he realized it was time he apologized. Before he could get out a word, Marsha spoke again.

"Wait, you never answered my question. I saw the way you were looking at Jeremy when we walked in. Are you okay?"

Marvin wiped his face and stroked the low-cut beard coating his jaw, remembering the incident with his oldest son. It seemed small, but Marvin knew it hinted at a bigger change going on in Jeremy than just his size.

"Marsha, has Jerermy been cussin' around y'all?"

She shrugged.

"I dunno. I usually try to tune him out. He's gotten even more terrifying this summer."

"So I've heard. I might needa remind him who I am and where I'm from." Marvin nudged Marsha with his elbow until she let out a giggle.

He managed to avoid the question again, but was he okay? When was the last time he asked himself that? Between the necessary business changes in his Maryland operation and getting things situated in Ocala, he had been running on responsibility alone. By all means, the family's essential needs were met. But with all of his life's current events, up until now, every time he spoke to one of his children he felt a familiar sense of foreboding.

The whole reason for lying in the first place was to work out all of the fine details of the move so he could make it smooth for the children. He worked out where they would live, transportation of their belongings, what schools they would go to, what doctors they would see for their sports physicals. He even talked to coaches to make sure the older two had spots at tryouts. And, of course, he had worked out what he would say when they asked him why.

Why did he lie? "Because I wanted you all to enjoy your summer," he would say. "I didn't want you to worry about any of this until I was sure I had the answers that would put your worry to rest." That was the plan. And man, did it backfire. Aside from issue after issue, and detail after detail that his brother left out of the initial briefing, the past three weeks wrenched him with tough criticism from the people who mattered to him most—his babies. Worst of all, no one had even asked the question. No one had asked him why.

There was no time to dwell, though. He had to clean and polish up the mess he'd made, plus, of course, his brother's.

Marvin had dropped Jacob off early that morning at Aunt Marybell's to meet Tre at the land. They wanted to look for the fabled cabin that their great-grandfather, Michael Cole Swallowtail Sr., was said to have built.

Its location was lost on the expansive forty-seven acres, but somewhere deep inside, Marvin thought maybe, if they found the cabin, they would find the deed. His heart sank when he pulled up to the access road and found Tre stomping on a padlock on a makeshift fence that the city had put up. A large red and white NO TRESPASSING sign was fastened to the gate. After talking his brother down, Marvin realized the process of getting the land back was going to be much more complicated than he thought. Everything about this move was becoming much more complicated than he thought.

"I learned a lot about our family today ... well, mostly about Grandpa Mikey," Marsha recounted.

"Ahhh, your momma took you to Loretta's didn't she?"

"Yes! I loved it! I didn't know Grandpa was a contractor like you! He basically built half of Ocala!"

"Ha, not that much, only this side of town. But yup, my pops was one of the best contractors around. He taught me everything I know. And not just about how you build buildings. A big part of a contractor's job is building relationships—strong ones, and keeping them."

"Were you close to him?"

"Something like that." Marvin smiled at his daughter. "Either way, he was the best man I know."

"Why don't you talk about him a lot? Or Grandma? Or anyone else in our family? Mrs. Loretta said the Swallowtails have been here for more than three generations."

Marvin took a deep breath in and let it out with a sigh.

"That's a very good question, Marsha. I don't know if I have a good answer. Our relationship was complicated."

"Well, does it have something to do with why you and Mommy

left Ocala?"

Marvin was used to Marsha's pressing questions. She was a curious little girl from the moment she could talk, and Marvin especially loved feeding her curiosities. She came by them honestly. As she grew older, they embarked on thought experiments, unpacked social topics, and discussed politics, never straying away from the tough issues. Around strangers, she liked to stay quiet and listen more than she spoke, holding her opinion until someone, usually Marvin, asked her. In contrast, around people she was comfortable with, his daughter was a fierce debater, making connections and pointing out fallacies with ease. It made him so proud, even when he was her target.

Again, Marvin let out a deep, full sigh and readjusted himself on the couch.

"No. Things were tricky with Pops and me but that's a story for a different time. Your mother and I left Ocala because I couldn't find it in my heart to forgive my brother. Right now, he needs me, so I don't have room to think too much about why I shouldn't be there for him. I ... I have no other choice."

Marsha sat with this for a second.

"I was thinking ..."

"Uhh oh ..." Marvin joked and was happy to see his baby girl find entertainment in it.

"I was really upset at you and Mommy for not telling us we were moving. But I know that if you didn't tell us, there was probably a good reason. I'm sorry for how I've been acting. I know this probably hasn't been easy for you either."

"Oh baby girl, you have nothing to apologize about. I apologize. From the bottom of my heart." Marvin gently squeezed his daughter's shoulder.

"I apologize for lying, for uprooting your life, and for the situation I put you in with Abby. To be honest, I never thought we would move back here after we left. But I forgot the most important lesson my dad taught me—Swallowtails are strongest when we're together."

Marsha snuggled closer under her father's solid frame.

"Will Uncle Tre be okay?"

"I don't know, baby," he said, squeezing his arm around her shoulders. "But I hope so."

"I am excited for school to start. After hearing all of Mrs. Loretta's stories I want to know more about Ocala. More about where our family is from. I just have to tell Abby."

"I'll tell you what. Call her up, I'll sit right here with you."

Marsha smiled, then reached for her phone.

The phone call with Abby went well, and Marsha was happy she had her dad there to help her through. Although both girls were sad, they agreed to meet in Disney when Abby and her family visited over Christmas. For the first time in a long time, Marsha went to bed feeling happy. Nestled on her mattress that now had a bedframe, she snuggled under her covers and began mentally planning her outfit for the first day of school until she drifted off to sleep.

When Marsha awoke, something about her bedroom seemed ... strange. The white light of the moon shone bright through her window, unlike the filtered light she had gone to sleep under. Marsha sat up and peeked out the window only to see that the forest she typically encountered was gone. Instead, a large field surrounded by forest on three sides took its place. In the center of the field stood the small shadow of an oak tree with a flicker of light illuminating its silhouette like a halo.

The Traverse, she thought to herself.

VI

"Uncle VanDyke? Are you there?"

No answer.

Marsha laid back down and pulled the covers over her shoulders. She thought she might just go back to sleep, but her curiosity overtook her fear. Marsha swung her legs over the edge of the bed and into her slippers, twisted into her robe, and slid out of the window. She still wore her silk scarf tight over her fresh braids.

It took a few minutes for her eyes to adjust to the pale darkness cast by the Traverse's moon. She struggled to see the pathway towards her family tree over the thick patches of young sabal palms and beautyberry bushes—clumps of berries ranging from a vibrant fuchsia to lemon green clustered on the wiry branches. For a moment, she thought she might be lost, but just then, she heard the high-pitched siren of a bird just above her head. When she looked up, she saw a single swallow-tailed kite circling above her. Gliding on the thermals, the raptor used its distinctive V-shaped tail to perform subtle acrobatics with the grace of a summer's wind. Swooping down low, the bird called again, its screech far from piercing, but still penetrating enough to feel the song in the tone. Something in Marsha resonated with the sound. Instead of being alarmed by the bird call, like she usually was, she felt at ease. Accepting it as a sense of familiarity, Marsha spoke to the bird.

"Hello! Can you help me get to the tree?"

Marsha listened as the bird screeched, but no words came out like when she met Uncle VanDyke. It swooped down low again, drawing figure eights in the shadowed sky. Marsha took a step forward, and the bird swooped back up, breaking the pattern, before flying forward. It continued its path, being sure to stay in Marsha's sight while she broke through the sabal palms onto patches of wildly overgrown Spanish needle. Marsha moved intently, her head swiveling up for directions, and down to watch for dangers. She wasn't sure if the typical Florida wildlife roamed the Traverse like they did in her real world. If so, snakes, scorpions, and even alligators could be hiding anywhere. She relaxed a little when she noticed there weren't any mosquitos or noseeums buzzing around her. Finally, the thicket opened into a field of native grasses, and there, standing regally in the middle of the field, was the Swallowtail family tree. It wasn't busy with birds this time. As a matter of fact, the only bird she saw was the one that led her there.

Marsha hurried to the back side of the tree to check on the fire. There it was, slowly burning deep in the thick of the branch. Its rays casted shadows through the leaves like a large candle in the stained glass window of a church.

The kite swooped around the tree and landed on the hill of a branch that, just beyond its thin black talons, dipped close enough to the ground for Marsha to sit on. She took the spot and stared at the bird, leaning back on the branch, which curved in the shape of a swing. For a moment, there was nothing but stillness.

"So ... Do I know you?"

The bird simply blinked.

Marsha sighed and tilted her head back on the branch.

"If God wanted me to get over my fear of birds, he could have sent me to the zoo."

The bird screeched loudly, as if responding in displeasure.

Marsha sighed and scanned the canopy of the tree. The branches moved and curved like they were dancing under the stars. It was quiet. All she could hear was a gentle rustle of wind through the leaves and the faint crackling of the fire on the far side of the tree. Something was different from the last time she was here. Where were all of the other kites? Suddenly, all of the questions from that first night rushed back into her mind. How was she going to put this fire out? How did it all connect to the land or her Uncle Tre?

Marsha stood up in frustration.

"Well, I'm here ... What am I supposed to do now?"

The bird sidestepped an inch closer to Marsha, causing her to flinch and take a step back.

It blinked again, then took to the sky, flying just over Marsha's crouched body.

Birds. Of all the cool things I could have been able to talk to ... it had to be birds.

She found the kite circling over the edge of the field to the left of her family tree. As she approached, Marsha found a trailhead bending into the forest. Something about the trailhead looked familiar, like the one at the park Aunt Marybell would take them to during the summer if it wasn't too hot. She had never gotten the chance to explore it, but she did see a girl that looked about her age entering it the last two times she was there.

The bird called again and Marsha built up the courage to follow. For a moment, she could see the bird steadily soaring high above through the break in the canopy, but soon, the trail thinned and the treetops began to lean together blocking out the sky. She could no longer see the bird, and panic began to knock on her heart.

"Okay. That's about as far as my curiosity will take me ... it's way too dark out here for this," Marsha thought out loud, somewhat hoping the bird would hear her and reappear. She turned around to head back down the trail, but to her surprise, it was gone. In its place was a dark, thick forest, disorientating Marsha. She turned around again and found herself under a veil of muscadine grapes, Spanish moss, and young trees.

Quick, heavy footsteps were approaching behind her and Marsha crouched down low to stay out of sight. Her heart was beating so hard that she thought it might give away her location. It hadn't registered to her that there might be other people in the Traverse. Peering through the holes between the grapevines, Marsha caught a glimpse of a small cabin and a tall, dark man hurrying inside. He emerged with a small box in one hand and a rifle in the other, and ran towards the field. From the other side of the cabin, Marsha heard more footsteps, but this time, they were fast and plentiful. And they came with voices. Angry voices. Shouting voices. And torches streaking through the forest without concern for where the embers fell.

Marsha clasped her hand over her mouth to silence her gasp, and tried to hold back the fearful tears in her eyes.

"It's my dream, I'm in control. It's my dream, I'm in control," she quietly repeated the words Uncle VanDyke and her father gave her, while the mob got closer and closer. As thick as the smoke was in the air, it was nothing compared to the dense hatred the mob carried with it. She had no idea where the man went and she didn't care. She just wanted to be home. Suddenly, all of the smoke, yelling, and footsteps vanished, and everything around Marsha was calm, once again.

When Marsha opened her eyes, she was in her room, crouching beneath her window.

Without thinking, she ran to her parents' room. Her mother was fast asleep but her father turned over and squinted at her standing in the doorway.

"What's wrong baby?" he said, still trying to wake himself up.

"I ... I don't know. It was a dream."

Marvin nudged Yonna trying to wake her up, but was unsuccessful. He looked at Marsha, who was also confused. Normally, Yonna couldn't sleep through a pin drop, but she seemed completely unphased by either of their attempts to pull her from sleep. Marsha walked over to the window expecting to see the thick young forest she had grown used to during the daytime. Instead, however, just past the low growing shrubs, Marsha saw the clearing, the large live oak, and the glow of fire coming from its burning branch. It was bigger now than when she left it, and this scared her even more.

"I'm still in the Traverse ..."

"The what?"

"Daddy, what do you see when you look out of the window? Does it look different to you than it looks during the day?"

Marvin joined her at the window and peered into the distance.

"Well, that's interesting. Marsha, what is going on?"

From there, Marsha told her father everything. About the first dream when she saw Uncle VanDyke, about their family tree, and all of the swallow-tailed kites that lived in it. She left out no details, especially when describing the experiences of that night. Marvin listened, firm faced and stoic.

"Listen Marsha, I know this is strange and confusing ... but that's just how dreams are. And this is nothing more than that. That's why you were able to get back to your room just by wishing for it."

"Then how come you're in it too?"

"Again, because that's how dreams are. Listen to me ..." Unconcerned about waking Yonna, Marvin sat on the edge of the bed and pulled Marsha in front of him to look directly into her eyes. "If you're anything like the kind of dreamer I am, then your dreams come with strange messages that only our reality can explain. It's important to stay grounded in that. In the real world. Otherwise, you can get lost."

"But, Daddy! What if this isn't like our other dreams? What if Uncle VanDyke was right about the Traverse and what's happening here is because of what's happening in the real world? What if the Traverse holds the keys?"

"Did you hear what I just said to you? The keys are in the real world, baby! Listen. I don't want you traveling out there by yourself anymore. Understand me?"

"But—"

"Do you understand me, Marsha?"

Marsha scanned his face closely. He sounded angry, but what she saw looked much more like fear. Why would her father be afraid of this? Did he question her strength or wits? That was the only answer that made sense, the only possible explanation for him to believe Marsha didn't know the difference between a regular dream and *this*. And if he didn't believe she could do that, then why on Earth wouldn't he help her? She let out a deep sigh to hide the snarl attempting to wrinkle her face, and crossed her arms.

"Yes, I understand."

"Good," Marvin exhaled a deep sigh of relief. "I'll make us some chocolate milk, then it's time to go back to bed. You have a big day coming up."

"It's okay. I'm just gonna try to go back to sleep." Marsha shook her head and started towards the door, stopping just before the threshold. "Daddy, you didn't see what I saw. This isn't just a dream." She left the room before he could respond, closing the door behind her.

VII

Marsha navigated the crowded halls of Silver Springs Middle School. It was her first day of seventh grade, and despite the echoes of the angry mob and her dad's denial of it, her day was going pretty smoothly. Her plan was to get to each class early and sit in the middle of the row by the window. That way she'd stay out of the way—but not in the back corner, which could draw just as much attention to her as if she sat front and center, if not more. She was going to scope out the scene for a month or so, then maybe join a club.

Marsha was glad her parents insisted on bringing her for a tour before the school year started, so she didn't look like the sixth graders sputtering around the hallway in search of their locker or next class. She waded past the group of girls squealing and hugging each other and skirted through the long line hanging out of the girls bathroom. Arriving at second period before anyone else, Marsha headed to her predetermined seat under the window. Two students who had to be twins walked in behind her. The boy headed straight to the back of the room, and the girl bounced into the seat just in front of Marsha. More students started filing in, some waving goodbye to friends at the door, others bumping past and finding their seats without even looking up. Marsha didn't know anyone at her new school, but all day, she had been scanning faces to see if maybe the girl from the trailhead was a student there too.

"OMG!!" the overly excited twin squealed as the last student entered the room. Marsha looked up, and to her surprise, there she was. The trail girl. She wore a yellow tie-dyed T-shirt with the portrait of a black woman from antebellum times and jeans embroidered with honeycombs on the front pockets. Her shoes were black canvas sneakers with a word Marsha couldn't quite make out written in black marker on the sole.

"I'm so glad you're in this class!" Twin continued, voice still squeaking at a nearly painful octave. Trailgirl took the seat next to her, diagonally in front of Marsha.

"Girl, calm down," Trailgirl said, flashing a warm smile. "We planned this, remember?" Then she hugged Twin from across the aisle.

A tall, radiant woman walked through the door just before the final bell rang.

"Sorry about that y'all, I was helping out some sixth graders. They're worse than y'all were, and y'all were pretty bad."

"Ms. Arbor!" The room erupted in excitement as Ms. Arbor, their social studies teacher, greeted the familiar faces, then settled the class down for roll. Cleo Bell Moore was the trail girl's name, and Samira and Senai Omar were the twins.

Samira caught Marsha staring at Cleo and turned with a questioning glare. Marsha folded her lips into an awkward smile and looked down at her desk shyly.

"You're new?" the excited girl said, more as a statement than a question.

Marsha nodded. Cleo was looking in question now too, which made Marsha overly aware of how she sat in her seat.

"What was your name again?" Cleo said.

"I'm Marsha."

"I'm Cleo. And this is Samira."

"But everyone calls me Mira," Twin butted in.

Marsha smiled at the girls.

"Where'd you come from? I bet it was Middleton. You look like a Middleton girl."

Marsha didn't know what Middleton was or what made her look like she came from there.

"Uh, no. I'm from Maryland."

"Maryland? Like where the White House is?"

"No, that's D.C. It's really close though."

Mira mouthed a wide *OH* and nodded.

"I really like your shoes, and your hair. Did your momma do it?" Cleo asked.

"No, I got it done at a place called Loretta's."

"You know about Mrs. Loretta's?" Mira said with a scoff. "That place is so ghetto!"

"Mira, don't be rude," Cleo said. "I've never been to Mrs. Loretta's shop. My momma's always done my hair. But from what I can see, they do really good work!"

Marsha smiled again and gently swirled a braid in her finger.

"Are both of you from Ocala?" she asked.

"Born and raised!" Cleo said proudly.

"Yeah, we've known each other since pre-K. She's my ride or die."

"Girl, what are you talking about? I'm not getting into no mess where riding or dying are my only options."

Mira laughed a little too loud for the joke.

"Clee-Clee you know you'd do anything for me!"

Cleo rolled her eyes but smiled in amusement.

"Mira, I have told you so many times. Please don't call me that."

"But you need a nickname!"

"A nickname is supposed to be shorter, and my name is already short. Anyways, Marsha, let us know if you need anything at all. I know this school is big, but we've known most of these kids since diapers. We got you."

"Ladies," Ms. Arbor interrupted. She stood at the front of the room with one eyebrow raised.

"Sorry Ms. Arbor, we were just getting to know the new girl."

"That is very on brand, Samira. And also very kind. Marsha, I can't wait to learn more about you with our first project."

"Project?" Mira complained. "Already? We haven't even learned anything yet!"

"Yes ma'am, your family tree project."

Marsha's ears perked up. Family tree project? What were the odds that the topic of her first project on her first day of school mirrored that of the strange and undeciphered dreams she began having the moment she discovered Ocala was her new home? It could have been a coincidence, but Marsha didn't believe in those.

"Social studies," Ms. Arbor explained, slowly pacing up and down the rows of her classroom, "is the study of individuals, communities, systems—and their interaction among time and place. It's like a road map of society, how it became what it is from what it used to be. But I think about it like this—just like any history, social studies depends on perspective. *Your* perspective. If this class is a road map, then you are the starting point." She met the eyes of what seemed like every student in the class, stopping at Marsha to complete her sentence. "If you don't know where you are, then how will you ever figure out where you're going?"

Ms. Arbor continued her pacing until she reached the front of the room once more.

"In this case, *where* you are is synonymous with *who* you are. So, we will start our studies by diving into who you are. Each and every one of you. And we will do so by making a family tree. Who were the people that came before you? What were they all about? How do they influence who sits in this classroom today?"

Ms. Arbor wove a thread of inspiration through every student in the room, especially Marsha. After she gave a few more directions and handed out the rubric, Ms. Arbor instructed the class to pick their partners.

For a moment, Marsha looked dreadingly at all of the students partnering up with familiar faces. Abby had always been her go-to partner and although she was having a pretty good first day, her heart ached now more than ever. Before the feeling could take root, Cleo turned to Marsha.

"Hey, wanna be my partner?"

"But ..." Mira wined.

"It's a family tree project, Mira. Don't you think you should do it with Senai ... your *twin* brother?" Cleo said, pointing at a skinny, dark haired boy with a shadow of hair on his upper lip making his way to their side of the room.

"Oh, yeah. I guess that does make sense."

"So, Marsha? Wanna discover who we are, together?" Cleo swayed her body slightly as her eyes widened in staged excitement as she repeated Ms. Arbor's words.

"Yeah, sure!"

Marsha hadn't expected to make friends so soon, but the girls were so nice and welcoming, even with Mira's sporadic outbursts. Although her plans to lay low were shattered, the resistance inside of her gave way and she realized that this is what Mrs. Loretta was trying to tell her. As badly as she wanted to, Marsha couldn't hate Ocala anymore. It was embracing her, and she was going to let it.

Ms. Arbor led the class to the library to begin researching. Cleo and Marsha found a computer towards the back of the room.

"Do you wanna start with your family?" Marsha asked, fingers ready to type into the search engine.

"We can, but there's not much to research to be honest. My mom was adopted, and my dad is really big on honoring our ancestors."

"No way, my mom was adopted too! But what do you mean, honoring your ancestors? Like how the Native Americans did?"

Cleo slowly nodded her head, considering.

"Yeah, pretty much. We can trace his side back like seven generations, and we recite the family names every morning when we pray to thank them for what they passed down to us. We start with the Moores. That's my family. We go all the way back to Spain. Then there's the Freemans, the Johnsons, the Hughes, and the Forresters. My grandma married a Forrester. They were one of the first free black families in Florida. The Briskers, the Monroes, and the LeBruns are all from Louisiana ... girl, the list goes on and on. "

"Wow, and y'all do that every morning? Why?"

"Well, it's kinda like Ms. Arbor said. My dad says, 'you have to know your own history or the world will try to tell you who you are.'" Cleo made her voice deep, impersonating her father. "And honestly, my dad is right. Last year the band teacher tried to tell me the only successful black musicians in early America were blues and jazz artists. I told him he was loud and wrong, so he told me to prove it. Search for Franklin Johnson from Philadelphia."

Marsha searched the name and the first link read *Franklin Johnson, the greatest composer you've never heard of.*

"See. That's my great-great-great-uncle ... or is it great-great-great-great-uncle?" Cleo counted generations on her fingertips. "Either way ... he was one of the first Americans to tour Europe in 1838. And if I didn't know his name and who he was, I wouldn't have been able to tell the band teacher just how loud and wrong he was. But enough about my family. What do you know about yours?"

"Definitely not that much ... Nowhere near that much. Aside from my Aunt Marybell and Uncle VanDyke, I don't know much about my family at all. The most I learned about my grandfather came from Mrs. Loretta when I was getting my hair done. Apparently he was her husband's best friend. But she did say something about my family being here for a long time, and how people would be willing to help me just because of my last name. But I still don't know anything about them."

"Well, let's start there then. What's your last name?"

"Swallowtail. Like the butterfly ... or the bird," Marsha answered, rolling her eyes to herself. "My grandpa's name was Michael, but everyone called him Mikey."

Cleo typed the information into the search bar. The first few links were old articles outlining her Uncle Tre's football career.

"Is that your dad?" Cleo asked.

"No, that's my uncle, his twin brother. My dad's name is Marvin."

"Wait, they're twins, but only one of them is named after your grandpa?"

Marsha nodded.

"How does he feel about that?"

"Well considering I can count on one hand how many times I've actually met my uncle, not too great."

"I bet," Cleo chuckled.

As the girls scrolled, their topic shifted to Michael Cole Swallowtail Jr. and his work as a contractor. The girls opened one webpage to a large image of Marsha's grandparents standing in front of Mrs. Loretta's shop. The headline read *Swallowtail breaking barriers for Negro businesses in Ocala.* There were a lot of people in the photo, lined up and smiling in front of the shop. Looking closely, Marsha saw a young Ms. Ne standing next to Mrs. Loretta, and a tall man with a thick mustache who she assumed to be her husband. Mrs. Loretta was holding a large pair of scissors aimed at the red banner positioned in front of the shop's door. Next to them was a man holding on tight to a stunning dark skinned woman with high cheekbones and big curls. The woman gazed up at the man, pride shining through her face, while he looked directly into the camera's lens. With broad shoulders and a low trimmed beard, the man looked like a photocopy of her father. But it was his wrinkled eyes that Marsha could spot from a mile away. They shone with pride too, but there was more to them. A certain regret tainted their inner corners and the wrinkles bent like a frown.

"Wow, this must've been the opening day of Mrs. Loretta's! She told me my grandpa and her husband built the plaza her shop is in and a bunch more like it. Apparently they only sold to black businesses."

"That's really cool! I wonder how many of the businesses are still open today?"

Marsha shrugged. The girls read a few more articles that all said similar things, praising the business, but there was not much else there.

"Wait, look at this!" Cleo moved the cursor over a link that read *WANTED: Michael Cole Swallowtail Sr. Assault, battery, and eluding arrest.*

The girls looked at each other in surprise.

"This must be your great-grandpa!"

"That's crazy, no wonder my family never talks about him."

Cleo carefully read the PDF copy of the old article.

"Hold on Marsha, something here doesn't sound right."

A great gathering has assembled on the 14th day of February, 1937 to locate Michael Cole Swallowtail Sr. for the purpose of fulfilling a warrant for his arrest. The warrant was issued after Swallowtail, a Negro man, brutally battered Thomas Guard, son of Colonel Isaac Guard, following a dispute over land ownership. The disagreement arose after Swallowtail refused to disclose the deed to his allegedly owned property on the northeastern side of town. Guard firmly believes that the Negro man and his family reside on stolen property and, in just service to his city, demanded that Swallowtail provide proof of ownership or vacate the property immediately. In retaliation, Swallowtail unleashed a wave of violence on Guard, in typical fashion for the likes of his kind. He then fled the scene and has yet to be accounted for.

"The likes of his kind?" Marsha snapped, rolling her neck in annoyance.

"You see what I'm saying! This doesn't sound right." Cleo continued reading the article, keeping her voice low beneath the light chatter of the rest of the class scattered about the library.

Colonel Guard and the white citizens of Ocala call for a search party to hand over Swallowtail to the authorities so justice can be served. However, the Marion County Sheriff's department warns that Swallowtail may be armed and dangerous, and henceforth urges citizens to act in regard to their own well-being, with the preservation of their lives in mind.

The image of the dark man running through the woods from the angry mob flashed across Marsha's consciousness.

"There's no way," she whispered to herself.

"There's no way what?" Cleo asked.

Remembering where she was, Marsha looked Cleo in the eye, and pondered telling her about her dreams. She hadn't talked to anyone about them besides her dad, and that did nothing but re-dig a hole in their relationship that they had just started filling.

"It's nothing ..."

"You know something. I know you do. And you can't lie to me. I'm psychic and intuitive!"

"Oh yeah, then what is it that I know?"

"C'mon, you know it doesn't work like that ... but tell me! Did Mrs. Loretta mention something about this? Do you think your family is covering something up?"

"No, nothing like that. I ... this story just reminds me of a dream I had the other night."

"Oooooooh! I love interpreting dreams! What happened?"

Ms. Arbor bought Marsha a second when she stopped to check on the girls. Luckily, Cleo had clicked back to the webpage on Mikey Jr.

"Is that your relative?" Ms. Arbor said, pointing at the screen.

"Yes, it's my grandfather."

Ms. Arbor shook her head with a smile on her face.

"I should have known. I went to school with your parents, and your grandfather built the house I grew up in. Wow. Now that I think of it, you look just like your daddy. What a small world it is. Do me a favor, tell your parents Ashley Arbor said hello."

Marsha smiled and nodded okay, hoping Cleo had forgotten about their previous conversation. But as soon as Ms. Arbor was out of range, her new friend picked up right where they left off.

"Look, I know you just met me, but I might be able to help you find out what really happened to your great-grandpa! And I promise I'll keep it a secret if that's what you want! Ask Samira. I'm the best at keeping secrets."

"That's what everyone says right before they tell your secret."

"You've got a point, but if you can't tell, I'm not like everyone."

Cleo was right. Marsha had always been a great judge of character. She could tell Cleo was different. Not in a bad way, but in the same way Marsha knew she was different herself—in a way that urged her to trust Cleo.

"Fine," Marsha said with a sigh, and told Cleo everything. When she was done, she held her breath, waiting for Cleo to call her crazy and ask Ms. Arbor if she could switch partners. To her surprise, however, a large smile bloomed on Cleo's face.

"That. Is. Awesome!" Cleo whispered in excitement. "It must be so cool, traveling through the dream world ... I mean, the Traverse, right?"

Marsha's shoulders relaxed in relief as she nodded her head yes. Although she hadn't admitted it to herself, the conversation with her father did flicker a candle of doubt in her mind. Cleo looked like she genuinely believed her, but still, in that short moment, Marsha remembered that she really didn't know her. And Cleo seemed to know everyone. Maybe this was all a front. Maybe she had an expert poker face and by tomorrow, the whole school would know about the crazy new girl. Marsha's gut, on the other hand, said otherwise, and she decided to trust it again.

"You promise you won't tell anyone?"

"Duhh!"

"I dunno, it honestly feels pretty normal. I wake up like I would any morning, but instead of seeing the sun, or my baby brother jumping on my bed, it's still dark, and the view from my window is completely different. Once you're outside, everything is the same except the wildlife. I haven't seen anything other than the birds. Not even noseeums! Which is a blessing. I hate those things. And then there's the shapeshifting thing ... that's pretty interesting." Marsha paused, still considering.

"I lucid dream a lot," Cleo revealed, filling the gap in the conversation. "Like, when I dream, I know that I'm dreaming. But I can't make decisions and stuff like you can. Wait, so how does all of this relate to your great-grandpa?"

"I'm not sure, but as soon as we finished reading the article about him, the dark man running through the forest ... the mob ... it all came back to me." Marsha looked past Cleo for a moment, then shook her head, trying to make sense of everything.

"I mean, that would make sense, right? ... Just like the kite guided you to the tree, maybe it guided you to a clue as well?"

Marsha thought about this for a moment.

"That does make sense, but why me? What am I supposed to do with a clue like that, especially if my dad doesn't believe me? I barely know anything about my grandpa, let alone my great-grandpa."

"I'll be honest, this is a little beyond my personal dream interpreting experience. But I might know somebody who could help us find out! What are you doing this Saturday? Can you meet me at the park?"

"The park? What's there?"

"Aunt Chi," Cleo said, as her smile turned from curious to devious.

"Aunt Chi?"

"Yes, Aunt Chi. She's not my aunt, that's just what everyone calls her. She's a priest of some sort, and she does all different kinds of readings and divination. My dad has gone to her before about ancestors that we didn't know about. And every time, the information she gives us turns out to be true. She has a crystal shop that's open some Saturdays, right there on the corner. You just have to catch her when she's there. No one really knows where she lives, we just know it's somewhere deep in those woods back there."

"That's what you were looking for when I saw you at the park this summer, huh?"

"What? You saw me?"

"Yeah! A couple of times actually. When I was at the park with my siblings. I recognized you as soon as you walked into class."

"And ... when were you gonna say something?"

"As soon as it wouldn't make me seem like a stalker ..."

"Touché."

Marsha slumped in her chair. Any other time she would have shared Cleo's excitement over the possibility of uncovering a mystery. But this one hit close to home. Her most recent dream was frightening enough but now, after reading the article, she wasn't sure if she was ready to find out what really happened to Michael Cole Swallowtail Sr. And she definitely wasn't sure if she was ready to go asking some strange priest lady about it.

"Okay," Marsha finally answered. "I'll go. But only if we promise to leave it alone, and focus on your part of the project until then. This ... this is enough for me today."

"Fair enough," Cleo shrugged, and for the rest of the period, the girls planned out Cleo's family tree.

Before the class left the library, Marsha navigated back to the photo of her grandparents in front of Mrs. Loretta's. After zooming in as close as she could on the couple, she printed the photo. A hole in her stomach widened as she gazed into it. How could she miss people she had never met? She loved her family—even Jeremy—so badly that it hurt, and she had always been happy with just them. But now she knew there was more to the Swallowtail story than the six of them, and this man staring back at her seemed to be begging her to find it out. To make sure his story wasn't lost to time. Marsha folded the paper up and carefully slid it into her pocket.

VIII

Marvin felt Yonna tap her thumb on his hand, drawing his attention to the tightening fist he had formed around hers. The morning had started off trying. Marvin awoke to Marsha's yells, Jeremy's laughter, and an entire load of laundry dyed pale pink. It turned out that one of Jeremy's red athletic socks mysteriously ended up in a pile of white clothes. His son swore up and down it was a complete accident, but somehow, none of his clothes were in the load to be ruined. Then, upon Yonna's suggestion, Tre came over for breakfast with the family, since they would be accompanying him to his doctor's appointment anyway. Marvin tensely muscled through the stage act his brother put on for the children, pretending to be all cool, calm, and collected, and ignoring the fact that he was sick at all. The children, especially Jeremy, effortlessly gravitated to him, and Marvin couldn't blame them. Tre was a cool dude on the surface. He was funny and clever, and had endless stories of growing up in Ocala as a star running back on their high school football team. He conveniently left out the part about Marvin being the quarterback and captain of the same team, but Marvin kept his thoughts to himself. His children had already heard Marvin's perspective and he didn't need to prove himself to them, or to his brother. All anyone had to do was look around to see which of the twins had come out on top. It was the sly, backhanded compliments that were really getting to Marvin.

"Of course your father would have told the story better than I could if y'all had stayed in Ocala."

"Yeah, you know maybe you should tell them the story of why we left?"

At that, Tre used his charm to quickly change the subject, and luckily, Marvin's passive-aggressive backlash went unnoticed by the children.

Now, he and Yonna lingered in the small waiting room of the doctor's office while Tre's oncologist, a family friend named Derrick Coleman, ran some more tests. Subtle and effective was his wife in moments like this. Moments when he needed to hold back his instinct and remain poised while his palms sweat, his chest tightened, and everything in him wanted to panic. He loosened his grip and she thanked him with a gentle squeeze before reaching in her purse to answer a call.

"Baby, this is Marsha. I'ma step outside, okay?"

Marvin nodded, leaning back in his chair, trying to let the smooth jazz relax him. Just being in the same vicinity as Tre tugged at Marvin's nerves. "A little cancer." The words stammered over the music, festering the brewing resentment Marvin felt towards Tre. This was not "a little" cancer. It was liver cancer, and although the prognosis was positive, it was "big" enough for him to ask Marvin to uproot his family, risk the success of his business, and take time out of his Saturday morning for this doctor's appointment. Worst of all, it was "big" enough for Marvin to dream of

Tre's death several times since he first did at the beginning of the summer. This was Tre's problem. He always took life as a joke and had no concern for how his recklessness affected others. Now, here he was, spending his day in the doctor's office instead of what they really should have been doing—looking for the deed. Marvin tried to tame his irritation. He tried not to blame his brother for his condition. He was, however, a man of logic and principle, and liver cancer didn't come from nowhere. It came from years of drinking away his potential and finding subpar solutions at the bottom of a bottle. Tre had made his bed, but now everyone had to sleep in it.

The last thing Marvin wanted was for people to know the truth of how he felt. Ocala was a small town, and word spread as quickly as a summertime storm rolling through. Everyone he had seen since he came back mentioned how kind it was for Marvin to come be with his brother, especially with their troubled history.

"It's a good thing you're doing, moving back here for your brother," Mrs. Marshall, his family's longtime banker, said when they met about transferring his business accounts.

The whole town had watched the boys grow up together, how Tre tormented Marvin and how Marvin scowled at Tre. And now they all had the same look in their eyes that said, "I hope Tre appreciates it this time."

Mrs. Marshall knew best of all, because outside of Yonna, Marvin, and Tre, she was the only one who understood what really went down. Their father had just died, and Marvin and Tre were working with Mrs. Marshall to invest their inheritance to open a new contracting company in his memory. Tre used a disagreement over the company's name as an excuse to back out of the deal, when in reality, he had withdrawn his portion and blown it away God knows where. When Marvin found out the truth, the betrayal cut deeper than anything Tre had done before. Deeper than courting Marvin's first middle school crush, Cierra Butler, or spiking his drink at a high school party. Not only did he betray Marvin, who was struggling to make ends meet with two toddlers and a newborn Marsha, but he betrayed their father, who wanted nothing more than to get his land and see his sons carry on his good work. Within a month, Marvin and Yonna had packed everything and moved to Maryland.

The door into the back of the office creaked and Tre emerged behind Dr. Coleman.

"Marvin Swallowtail, my man!"

Marvin forced a smile onto his face and stood to dap up their old high school classmate and closest thing to a best friend he'd ever had—outside of Yonna.

"I heard the rumors and I wasn't sure it was true. Especially when I didn't get a call. But I guess I shouldn't have expected one since you left without telling me, too."

"Yeah, I'm sure you'll tell me how you really feel at an even more appropriate time ..."

"Man, it's all love. Always has been and always will be. But you know I always gotta get my licks in," Dr. Coleman took a fighting stance and threw two fake jabs at Marvin who threw his hands up in a fake defense.

"So, what's the word, Tre?" Marvin said, turning to his twin who was fixing himself a glass of water from the office fountain.

"I don't know yet. Doc wanted to come get you before we went over everything."

"Tre you're a grown man. You couldn't just get the information and tell me about it?"

"Aye man, who you talking to?"

VIII

Dr. Coleman chuckled to himself, interrupting the intensifying moment.

"I see not much has changed, even after almost two decades. Listen Marv, I suggested Tre bring you along with him today for a few reasons. We'll discuss it all in my office."

Just then, Yonna reappeared. "Derrick Coleman, it's great to see you!" She hugged the family friend. "Thank you so much again for helping us with this."

"Oh it ain't nothing but a thing. These guys, as crazy as they get, were my roll dogs growing up. And I wouldn't be where I am today without Mr. Mikey. His company built this building. It's the least I could do."

"Everything okay with Marsha?" Marvin asked.

"Um, yeah. Can you ride back with Tre? I gotta go meet her up by the park. We'll talk about it later. How's everything here?" She met eyes with the other men, avoiding Marvin's questioning gaze.

"I was just about to take everyone back to my office. These two still can't be in the same room together for but so long, so I'll try to make it quick. Follow me this way."

Yonna shot the twins a look and pointed a finger back and forth between them. "Y'all better behave," she teased, then kissed Marvin goodbye.

Once in the office, Tre and Marvin sat in neighboring chairs before Dr. Coleman's desk. Dr. Coleman wasted no time explaining that Tre's cancer had progressed much more rapidly than usual and his tumor was growing, moving him into the stage two classification.

"Look, I'ma be honest with y'all," Dr. Coleman said in a compassionate, but serious, tone. "This is not going to be easy, and Tre, I'm not sure you realize how serious this is."

"I'm not worried Doc," Tre said, leaning back in his chair. "You said seventy percent of people survive this, right? I'm young, healthy, and have no other serious health concerns … so those odds seem pretty good to me."

"That was before your cancer progressed. For stage two, that number drops to about thirty-five percent. We gotta come up with a whole new treatment plan and start ASAP. And Tre, you'll need all of the support you can get."

The mood in the room tightened. Tre took a sharp breath in and clenched his jaw. Marvin felt his palms sweating again and took in the same short, sharp breath.

"He has that," Yonna would have assured. There was nothing more he wished for in that moment than to have her there.

"So what you're saying is, he gotta get his life together?" is what Marvin said instead.

"Well, we have a couple of options. We can start right away with chemoembolization, or targeted chemotherapy, to shrink the tumor …" Dr. Coleman paused and scanned the faces in his office.

"What's up, man? You know us, give it to us straight," Marvin said with an impatience you'd only catch after years of knowing him. His palms were now so damp they might have left a print on his shorts.

"Yeah, I know y'all. That's why I hesitate." Dr. Coleman let out a deep breath before continuing. "We can start with chemo. But from the looks of this thing and how it has already progressed, it's not gonna stop. It's not gonna just go away. Chemotherapy might shrink it, but Tre, you're gonna need a transplant. If we put you on the list, it could take months, even years to find a match. And, I'm serious Tre, you're gonna have to change the entire way you live your life. No more drinking. No more fried foods … It takes work. With that being said, waiting is not the only option." Dr. Coleman stopped again, and leaned into his folded hands, avoiding eye contact.

"A transplant," Marvin finished for him. "And as his twin, I'm the best chance for an automatic match."

"Yes. A living transplant donor is the best treatment option here, especially since y'all are twins. With this plan, that survival rate can shoot up as high as eighty percent."

"Alright, let's do the transplant!" Tre exclaimed.

"Slow down Tre, we need to discuss the risks for both parties."

"And I have to agree," Marvin said, more coldly than he had intended.

They both looked at him. Dr. Coleman, with an expression that said "I know that, but why would you say that?" and Tre, with clear shock and disgust.

"What do you mean the risks? I'm dying! What else is there to think about?"

"There are a number of things to think about, Tre ..." Marvin trailed off.

"Yeah? Like what?!"

"My wife. My four children. You know, people who might be affected if I made a risky decision without thinking about them!" Marvin answered, anger and frustration clenched between each word. He had tried his best for three weeks to keep his temper tamed, to remain poised. But at this point, all he could do to mask the tightening of his chest was let the anger drip out.

Tre twisted to meet Marvin's glare.

"I'm your brother! Your twin brother!" He let out a short, hard breath and the anger in his eyes changed to pain. Or was it desperation?

"I ... I understand it's a big deal, asking you, but what ... you plan to just let me die?" Tre's voice almost cracked as he spoke.

"Of course not," Dr. Coleman cut in, "I think we just need to get all the information disclosed before we make a decision." But Marvin had already looked away, and Tre had already seen him do it.

"You don't have to decide right now. We'll need to do chemo first to shrink the tumor regardless ..." Dr Coleman continued. But Marvin couldn't do it. He couldn't breathe anymore. He stood up too quickly, and the room shook.

"Where the hell you going?" Tre spit.

When Marvin dreamed of his parents' death, he was a helpless observer, as if he were stranded on the wrong side of a one-way mirror. Plus, those dreams weren't recurring. This was not the case when he awoke to Tre's fate, night after night. Tre could see him. Could reach for him, and Marvin could reach back. Sometimes he did. Sometimes he'd reach for Tre, try to pull him out and save him in vain. Other times, despite the amount of shame it brought him, Marvin did nothing. Those nights, he wished it would just happen, instead of dragging it out through radiation, surgery, or whatever Tre was going to need. Sometimes he wished Tre would just ... go.

He knew it was wrong, that's why he showed up. That's why he kept showing up. But this was more than showing up, and again, Tre's only concern was himself. Anyone else would at least have the thought that just maybe, after already moving, sacrificing himself would be asking too much. Not Tre. Tre had all the audacity. Still, Marvin felt he had no choice. How would he be able to live with himself if his only brother died because he decided not to do the one thing that could save him?

"See?" Tre said, but his voice sounded distant and faint. The light dimmed under the amplifying drum of Marvin's own heartbeat. Its pace increased rapidly, and a sharp pain tore through his temple. He tried to ask for water, but when he opened his mouth to speak, the knot in his chest wrung itself tighter, clogging his throat. His jaw trembled as he gasped for air and the room around him became a blur of colors. The last thing he heard was Tre's voice, distant and muffled.

"You always running. Just like Dad said."

Then everything went black.

IX

MARSHA SAT ON THE BENCH THEY HAD DECIDED to meet on and texted Cleo that she had arrived. After the first day of school, the girls realized they lived in the same neighborhood and began walking home together. The chosen bench was where they sat each afternoon, unpacking the day's events, debating which bugs were the most annoying, and feeling like they had known each other their whole lives before departing down the streets that led to their homes. The bench was far on the other side of the playground, closer to Cleo's street, towards the back where the walking trails were. To Marsha's relief, the park was empty for a Saturday. Only one family chased each other around the playground, and a couple of older boys played basketball way up by the entrance that she had come through. Marsha was far enough away from both to find some peace and quiet.

She slouched low on the bench and leaned back. Of course, as soon as she looked up, a swallow-tailed kite glided over the tops of the trees into her sphere of sight. For a moment, she watched it dip and dive, showing off its agility in the sky above her, before perching itself on a high branch some yards away.

"I read about you, you know. You're not even supposed to be here. The rest of you have already taken off down south for the winter. They're probably flying over the Nazca Lines or resting in Brazil nut trees in the Amazon as we speak. So tell me, bird, why have you decided to stay and torment me?"

The bird took off again, continuing its acrobatic performance, unbothered by Marsha's inquiry. Marsha rolled her eyes. She was already feeling uneasy about the visit to Aunt Chi's, and the bird seemed to have no other business there other than mocking her. Her morning had gotten off to a rough start. Her father was more high strung than he had ever been, and her mother was clearly worried out of her mind. Jeremy was getting meaner every day, and Marissa, when she was actually home, spent most of her time locked in her room. Worst of all, their uncle came by that morning with a notice from the city saying they had less than thirty days to locate the deed to the land. She was watching her family fall into a sort of disarray, and although she had no idea how, Marsha knew it was all tied to the slowly burning oak tree in her dreams. The fire she had been tasked with putting out. The tree she was responsible for saving.

Marsha let her head fall back and closed her eyes. She tried to conjure up reasons why her parents, or even Aunt Marybell, never spoke about their family, and why she had been reluctant to ask in the first place. She could blame it on her father's dismissal of her dreams, but that wasn't fair. Any other time he was willing to talk to her about any other subject—from God, to boys, to stress, even politics—and her mother was the same way. They were straightforward and logical people, and she could usually depend on answers that were honest and complete. But when she considered asking them about their estranged family, her stomach twisted into a knot of uncertainty. She saw the way her father and uncle acted in the same room, constantly bucking at one another in silent, discreet competition. Plus, her parents lied about moving back in the first place, and didn't seem to care much about preparing Marsha for what she was discovering now. So, what could she hope to get from them if she did ask? As if mirroring her bleak thoughts, the glow of the sun behind her closed eyelids dimmed and the temperature cooled. Marsha assumed a morning rain was brewing, but when she opened her eyes, the whole park had vanished and was replaced by thick woods, and a small clearing before her. The bench she relaxed on was there, but the metal frame was replaced by wood planks, and the asphalt sidewalk was now a thin dirt trail. Marsha stiffened in disorientation. For a brief moment, the scene looked familiar, as if she had been there before.

The kite sounded its high-pitched screech and the vision melted back into the scenery of the park. As she looked around in disarray, Marsha spotted Cleo approaching from the back gate.

"Hey girl, sorry I'm late. Are you ready? ... Are you okay?"

"Hey, Cleo."

There was hesitation in Marsha's voice, and the look on Cleo's face said she knew something was up.

"Are you okay?" Cleo asked again.

Marsha rubbed her eyes and took a deep breath.

"Yeah, I think so ... I dunno. The dreams are getting weirder and weirder."

"How so? What happened? Did you dream last night?" There was a slight excitement in Cleo's voice, but other than that, she looked genuinely concerned.

"Yeah, but I've already told you what's been happening when I do. No birds, no new clues, just me, sitting under the tree. Waiting for answers to fall from the sky." Marsha opened her palms to the sky, then let them flop to her side in a frustrated gesture.

"But this was different," Cleo guessed.

"Yes. This was different. Just a second ago before I saw you were here ... I closed my eyes and when I opened them I was in the Traverse."

"Wait, you mean like right here?"

"Yes!"

Cleo looked around as if searching for some sort of clue or remnants of the vision.

"I'm okay though," Marsha assured. "I'm probably just stressed. This is all turning out to be a lot. You remember my uncle I told you about?"

Cleo nodded.

"Well, I finally met him this morning ... well, re-met him, I guess. I was a baby last time he was around. Anyways, he came by for breakfast."

"So," Cleo questioned. "What was he like? Was he terrible?" During their week attached at the hip, both girls had become experts on all things regarding the other, and because of the project, family was the main topic.

"No, not at all surprisingly. He was actually pretty funny and really laid back. He's like the opposite of my dad to be honest."

"Yeah, if I didn't know better your dad would kinda scare me."

Marsha laughed at that. Her dad could be intense, but his level of restraint and poise was something she had always admired about him.

"Yeah, but they don't get along. And so my dad was upset. And I don't think he realizes but, when my dad's upset, everyone is."

"Girl, same," Cleo exhaled, shaking her head.

"And I know that it will get better as soon as I figure all of this out."

"Well, let's get going then. Hopefully Aunt Chi can give you some answers."

Marsha let out a deep sigh, got up, and the two headed towards the forest trail.

"I was thinking," Cleo began, breaking the silence. "My dad always tells us that our ancestors don't let us face any challenges we aren't prepared for. He says they always have our back. I don't think your dreams or visions are just because of stress. Your first dream happened the first night you moved here. The next one happened after you spoke to Mrs. Loretta. Maybe the clues only come when you're ready for a new one. I mean, it's very clear that you're being guided."

"Why do you say that?"

"Think about it. Mrs. Loretta knows your grandfather, Ms. Arbor is an old friend of your parents', your first project in her class is a family tree, and you randomly met me, the girl you saw walking to meet the woman who can give you all the answers you need. Don't you see? Your ancestors are guiding you in the real world just like they are in the Traverse! Man ..." Cleo stepped back, looking at Marsha with unfocused eyes, "It's almost like I can see them around you right now!"

"Hmm," Marsha thought, scanning the sky for the bird. "I don't really believe in coincidences. That's kinda why I agreed to come today. Too many things are lining up for them not to be connected."

"Well, I'm glad you did. I have a good feeling about this. Now, remember, this place might not be open. There aren't really any set hours. You kinda just have to catch her when you can. I'm thinking if Aunt Chi is there then that's just another sign that we're on the right track."

The girls rounded the corner at the back of their neighborhood to find an old wooden cabin painted white with a bright blue roof. The place looked ancient, but strong nonetheless. No cars were parked in the small pebbled parking lot. A small ramp on the side of the deck bordered three steps that led right to the front door. The sign, leaning on the inside of the decorative barred window, read *Aunt Chi's Rocks and Readings*. Cleo took the steps up to the front door while Marsha peered through the window in the center of the ramp.

"I don't see anybody inside."

When she turned to her friend, that same devious smile she'd dawned in the school library widened on Cleo's face as she held the door open.

"The door's unlocked, and the sign's turned to *Open*. It must be your lucky day."

Marsha rolled her eyes, but smiled and walked through the door with Cleo following close behind.

"Mr. Kwe! It's me, Cleo!" Cleo was peeking behind the desk towards a doorway draped with layers of patterned fabric. The inside of the store was massive compared to the small storefront, and the decor matched the aged charm of the outside. Marsha's eyes lit up as she looked around. When she was in fourth grade, she went through a period of rock obsession after her family visited the Grand Canyon, and could name many of the specimens on display in the shop. The rocks were all organized by color, starting with perfectly clear cut quartz all the way through iridescent, dark-rainbow labradorite. Each shelf was stocked with jewelry, baskets of rough stones, geodes, and more. The crystals themselves came in all shapes and sizes.

On the far wall, there was a bookshelf full of geology encyclopedias, color theory books, and crystal healing texts. Next to the bookshelf was a serving table with a vast array of tea selections. A couch and two lounge chairs, all upholstered with different fabrics and decorated with patterned pillows, anchored a thick Persian rug in the center of the room. Each piece, vintage and unique in its own way, seemed to fit together, as if they had only found their proper home when they found themselves next to each other on that rug. Mesmerized by her surroundings, Marsha slowly made her way to the bar-height counter where Cleo sat on one of three stools.

"Pretty cool, huh?" Cleo said proudly.

"I've been to rock shops before, but never anything like this. She has so many!"

Just then, an old man who looked to be about Aunt Marybell's age slowly emerged from the fabric curtains. He was tall, had a manicured salt and pepper mustache, and was dressed in a crisp, beige linen pants set. He wore a long, black tourmaline pendant wrapped in copper around his neck and several rings adorned the hand he used to grip his cane. The wooden handle was a carved figure Marsha couldn't quite make out.

"Cleo," the man greeted fondly in a deep, stentorian voice. "I thought I heard your voice. Chinara said you might be coming by today. And what is this, have you brought a friend?"

He didn't look at Marsha, instead the man simply tilted his ear in her direction. It was only then that Marsha noticed the frosted blue cloud over the man's pupils, and realized he was completely blind.

"I don't think I know that voice. Whom do I have the pleasure of meeting this morning?"

"This is Marsha! She just moved here from Maryland."

At first, Marsha only smiled, until realizing that he couldn't see her.

"Oh, hi."

She cleared her throat then cringed at herself while Cleo shook her head and giggled. The man smiled as well, then nodded his head in greeting. His small, single hoop earring caught a ray of sun and sparkled like the geodes on display behind the counter. He moved smoothly towards them, wearing a wise grin.

"Pleasure to meet you, Marsha. I'm Kweku, but you can call me Mr. Kwe. I make the jewelry here and keep the books."

HOW Marsha mouthed to Cleo, but Mr. Kwe answered instead.

"It's amazing how much more you can see without your eyes trying to guide the way." He flashed another cool, wise grin at her before continuing.

"Maryland, huh? I've never been but I heard it's real nice up there. How ya liking Florida so far?"

"It's okay. It got better when I met Cleo."

Cleo smiled at this.

"She does have that effect. Give it some time. It will grow on you. So," Mr. Kweku leaned one hand on his cane and the other on the counter where the girls sat, "what brings you ladies in today? Looking to add something to your collection?" Mr. Kwe winked at Marsha who was eyeing a geode on a shelf behind him. He lifted his hand and seemed to trace her gaze with it until landing on the hand-sized rock cracked open to reveal many angled crystal formations, all with clear bases that faded to a deep, striking blue on the tips.

"You know this one?" he asked.

"Is that ... sapphire?"

"It sure is. A beautiful stone, she is, with some amazing properties. What do you know of her?"

"Not too much, I read somewhere that some spaceships have windows made with sapphire because its score is nine on the Mohs scale ..."

"Ahhh, that's right. Did you know that it is practically fireproof as well? It can get to over thirty-five hundred degrees before melting." Marsha could tell he was excited from his tone, but the tight wrinkles on his face didn't shift from that same wise smirk. This man, Marsha decided, was the definition of cool.

"But I know you didn't come all of the way here from Maryland for this." Mr. Kwe turned towards Cleo and leaned on the counter once more.

"Well ..." Cleo said, dragging out the word just enough to cause Mr. Kwe to raise an eyebrow. "We're partners for a family tree project in social studies and ... we were hoping to get a mini-reading from Aunt Chi." Cleo flashed a pert, fabricated smile.

"A reading, huh? Do your parents know you're here?"

Both girls nodded. "It's not for me though, it's for Marsha."

Mr. Kwe pursed his lips and leaned deeper on the counter.

"Now Cleo, you know my wife won't do any readings on children without their parents present. But, I'll let her know y'all are here. Do you have your offerings?"

"Offerings?" Marsha looked at Cleo in confusion. "I only brought some cash for some crystals."

"Don't worry. Offerings can be literally anything that you find value in—money, art, you name it. But today, I got you." Cleo searched her bag for a moment and pulled out a white feather about the length of her hand with curved black stripes protruding from the rachis. "It's a white falcon feather! There's one nesting close to my backyard."

"Oh, Aunt Chi would love this! But, I'm afraid if the reading is for Miss Marsha here, the offering must be from her. It's an energy thing," Mr. Kwe explained apologetically.

"Oh, my bad Marsha, I didn't know that. Do you have anything with you at all?"

Marsha dug in her backpack. Sometimes she did keep an old stone or two in there from her collection, but she cleaned it out before school started. Plus, Aunt Chi probably already had tons of whatever stone Marsha would've provided. When the big pocket came up short, she checked the front and found the photo of her grandparents.

"This is all I have," Marsha admitted, trying to hide the shame in her voice.

Mr. Kwe ran his fingers over the photo with a curious look on his face.

"What did you say your name was again?"

"Marsha ... Marsha Swallowtail."

Mr. Kwe let out a deep, hardy laugh that filled the room.

"Well, I'll be. You don't need an offering, young lady. Y'all wait right here. Chinara will get a kick out of this."

Mr. Kwe handed the photograph back to Marsha and slowly left the room, muttering something to himself between chuckles. Cleo leaned over to whisper in Marsha's ear.

"I've never known Aunt Chi to do anything without an offering. Mrs. Loretta was right! From now on, when we need something, start with your last name!"

Marsha playfully rolled her eyes.

"Forget all that! How could he see the picture?"

"He's a blind jewelry maker and she's a rock collecting oracle. You gon' need to get used to some things just being what they are with these two, Marsha. Trust me."

"WHO?!" yelled a woman's voice from behind the draped doorway. "You better not be messing with me Kweku! You better not!"

The voice got louder and louder until the fabric flung open and a tiny old woman in a floor-length blue tunic stood in the frame. Although her energy was polar opposite of her husband's, the woman Marsha assumed to be Aunt Chi was the most magical-looking person she had ever seen. Her long dreadlocks were twisted with a white scarf around her head, easily adding a foot to her height. She wore thin wire earrings lined with various gems descending down until they brushed her shoulders. The tunic was embroidered with intricate designs at the hem, and her skin, deeply wizened and bare of makeup, seemed to glow in the late morning sun. Aunt Chi stood there, whimsical and fairylike, mouth open, for just a moment too long.

"Um, hey Aunt Chi," Cleo said, wearily glancing at Marsha, who awkwardly waved at the old woman.

That moment, Aunt Chi jerked out of whatever shock caught her and shook her head vigorously.

"Uh, uhhh! No way. You both better call your mommas right now. I am not doing this again! No, no, no! I have learned. My. Lesson." Aunt Chi bent over her thighs and slapped them with each word.

The girls looked at each other in question, then to Mr. Kwe, who was still chuckling to himself as he stood in the doorway.

"Uh, are we in trouble?" Marsha asked apprehensively.

"Trouble?" Aunt Chi kissed her lips and looked at the girls. "No, no, no. Listen, little birds. I know y'all don't know nothing 'bout nothing. But I also know y'all know there's something to know. I can tell from just looking atcha!"

"Huh?" Cleo murmured.

Marsha squinted her eyes trying to follow.

"Just listen to what I'm sayin'! Kwe told me y'all were working on a family tree project. You come here together, with this picture ... Y'all are snooping around things that get real deep, and real serious. About both of you." Aunt Chi stopped, looked both girls back and forth in the eye, then took a sharp breath and shook her head while continuing. "But they are not things that need to remain that way. So. I'm not saying a thing without the consent of both of your parents. Your mothers specifically."

Aunt Chi looked at the girls again, then waved her hand at them. "Well, go on ..."

X

Yonna spent the whole drive from Dr. Coleman's office kicking herself for missing that Marsha was going to Aunt Chi's shop. It was the only shop of that sort in their area and Aunt Chi had known Yonna for over four decades, so however Aunt Chi discovered who Marsha was, Yonna imagined her shoving a phone into Marsha's face to call. The old oracle was rather pushy at times. As with most people, she hadn't seen or spoken to Aunt Chi since days before she and Marvin fled Ocala all those years ago. It was easier for them to move on if they simply cut all ties. But this particular woman, with her humor, wit, and eccentricism, had been one of the harder relationships for Yonna to live without.

Yonna deeply missed Aunt Chi, so much so that as she entered the empty parking lot, she had to force away the tears forming in her eyes. She pulled the sun visor down to assess her appearance. "Whew. We're okay, right?" she asked her reflection, wiping away the last traces of the pesky tears. Her mascara was good, but her eyes ... her eyes were not her own. They were tired, worried—not the lively, optimistic gaze she was used to seeing on herself. One thing Yonna Swallowtail could do was hold it down, but in all honesty, she was exhausted. In the weeks since the family returned to Ocala, Yonna had been on damage control, making sure that Marvin could focus on Tre and the land, her children were settled and comforted, and the business back in Maryland remained successful. She was able to avoid the brunt of the recoil from the children while Marvin faced it all head on, ignoring that covert guilt lurking in the back of her mind. She saw the toll that weeks of putting her needs last was taking, and nervousness suddenly overcame any excitement or longing she felt about her pending reunion with Aunt Chi. She would only have to take one look at Yonna to see it all as clearly as the crystals in her shop.

What she hadn't considered was how difficult it would be to answer for their escape to all of the people they had left behind. The truth was, Yonna never wanted to leave Ocala in the first place. Tre had hurt her just as he had Marvin, and there was no doubt that at that time, he would have continued to do so. But everyone else they knew in Ocala had filled the positions of family she had never had. Marvin's love for her was more than enough to keep a smile on her face and there was nothing she wouldn't sacrifice for what they built together. But, their community—that family curated by the universe itself—she now realized was just as much of a necessity as was her marriage. It was the soil they were able to find their roots in. Everywhere she went—the grocery store, the post office, even the school—housed someone who had loved them, had been hurt by their departure, and had questions in the depths of their eyes. Luckily, instead of saying much, most people simply welcomed them home like the prodigal couple. A few who were closer to the family figured it had much to do with Mikey's death, and inquired further, albeit indirectly. Mrs. Loretta, with her all-knowing eyes, did things like look at her for half a second too long. She was sure Dr. Coleman had said something to Marvin, although likely through a signature passive-aggressive joke that somehow lightened the most serious conversations. None of them, however, showed any signs of holding grudges. And none of that made Yonna's guilt subside at all. If anything, she questioned if they deserved the love, the welcome, the help.

Another car pulled into the parking lot and parked a few spaces over. A woman, just about Yonna's age, hopped out and headed towards the door of the old cottage, probing Yonna to do the same. She was slightly taller than Yonna, and had a similar deep red tint beneath her copper skin as Marvin, which struck Yonna; the particular hue was what made the Swallowtail family so distinct. The woman flashed a radiant smile at Yonna and held the door open behind her. The smile, too, was familiar, albeit in a different way. It had a certain strength in its glow, one that had been scratched many times before, then buffed by graceful, yet radical resilience.

Inside, the shop looked exactly how Yonna remembered it, with the vast displays of rocks and outré decor. Marsha was sitting at the front desk reading a book next to a girl Yonna assumed was Cleo, her new friend from school. The other woman, based on how she pulled the girl close and kissed her, must have been Cleo's mother. Marsha greeted her mother then introduced her to Cleo, who introduced her mother, Gezie, to both of them.

Yonna looked behind the counter towards the fabric-covered doorway.

"So where's Mr. Kwe? Where's—"

"I'M COMING, I'm coming," Aunt Chi interrupted from the back room. "I'm just fixing y'all some tea!"

Yonna wished she would hurry up. She didn't know how long she had before Marsha started getting curious about how comfortable Yonna was in the space. As if reading her mind, Aunt Chi threw aside the partition, revealing herself, and once again, Yonna held back her tears. Mr. Kwe followed close behind with a tray carrying a beautiful blue tea set, chips, and fresh guacamole.

"Oh, stop your staring. Get over here and love on me."

The emotional look in Aunt Chi's eyes told a more sincere story than her blunt words. Yonna hurried behind the counter and sank into the woman's arms like a little girl. As tiny as Aunt Chi was, her expansive presence embraced every part of Yonna, comforting and soothing her entire being.

"You're home now, child!" Aunt Chi whispered in her ear. Yonna could almost feel Marsha blinking at them with curious intrigue, but she decided to keep the moment for herself. She blocked out the world and settled deeper into Aunt Chi's arms until her tears broke free. After the long, tender moment, Aunt Chi took Yonna by the shoulders and gave her a good look.

"Hmm," Aunt Chi let out a soft snort, "I see. We'll get this all fixed up in no time."

Yonna made no effort to try and understand. That was Aunt Chi's way—tiny, coded windows into her all-knowing mind. She was an oracle, after all. Yonna knew whatever Aunt Chi saw would be revealed soon enough.

Aunt Chi greeted Gezie while Yonna and Mr. Kwe had their own reunion. When she turned back to her daughter, Yonna could see confusion and curiosity all over Marsha's face. There was something else as well, a look that brought Yonna back to when Marsha was just a baby, trying to make sense of the world around her. Marsha's eyebrows furrowed, her bottom lip poked out slightly, and her head tilted towards her right ear. It had always been Yonna's favorite expression of Marsha's because it symbolized that the brilliant mind that she and Marvin created was hard at work. It was quite unnerving, however, to be the subject of her daughter's intense inner inquiry, and thankfully, Yonna was saved by Aunt Chi before Marsha could start asking questions. The old woman prompted everyone onto the couches to have a seat.

"I know y'all want to know what this is all about. Well, I'll tell you. This is business. Our business. And I promised myself if I ever got you all in the same room, I wouldn't hold back the truth! At the time, I didn't think that would ever happen, but ..." Aunt Chi cocked her head to the side as if speaking to herself, then rolled her eyes and shook the thought off in her amusingly dismissive way. "It has. And you all are here. Man, I need to cleanse my cards because they sure did not warn me of this today. Alright, well here goes. Marsha, Kwe told me you and Cleo are working on a family tree project at school. Did y'all know about this?" Aunt Chi directed this question to Gezie and Yonna.

"I believe Cleo mentioned something about it," Gezie said, growing anxious with anticipation.

"Well, let me tell you, God works in mysterious ways. I guess I'll just start from the beginning." With the guardianship of their mothers, Aunt Chi spoke directly to the girls. "I am the oldest of four cousins in my generation. Myself, Mikey, Marybell, and our youngest cousin, Marvin, who we all called Lil' Marv."

Marsha jerked her head towards her mother in shock, then to Cleo, whose eyes were as wide as her smile.

"Yes child, I am your great-aunt just like Marybell, but that is not the point here. Lis-ten! Goodness, you just like your daddy."

Yonna chuckled at this, then winked at Marsha, whose face curled back into question, but remained attentive.

"We were like siblings, the four of us. We all grew up right here in Ocala. Mikey and Marybell actually lived with me after their father went missing over that land."

Cleo shot Marsha a look at the mention of Michael Sr., which Marsha returned with a slight nod.

"We were so tight when we were young, the four of us, but Lil' Marv was a troubled man. A lot like your Uncle Tre is," Aunt Chi continued, nodding at Marsha. "As we got older, Lil' Marv found the dark side of Ocala and started making some really bad choices that really hurt our family. It was a difficult time for us all. Long story short, your grandfather, Mikey, was real hard on him. He wanted to cut him off completely. I wasn't ready to do that. I thought, even with all that he did, he still had some good in him. That boy," Aunt Chi's voice trailed off as she brought a hand to her lips. Mr. Kwe reached for her other hand and gently squeezed it in support.

"We all tried our best with that boy," Mr. Kwe said, finding the words where Aunt Chi could not.

"Well," she continued finally, "it had been about a year that Mikey and Sarah, your grandmother, were grieving the loss of a baby girl who didn't make it out of the womb. Lil' Marv showed up at their doorstep with a baby girl of his own. What a beautiful baby she was, couldn't mistake her for anything but a Swallowtail. The mother, let's just say she was not fit to parent that child and neither was Marvin. He left the baby with Mikey and Sarah, and we all pitched in to take care of her. Then one day, not too long after that, Lil' Marv came back, took the baby girl, and we didn't see either of them again. We found out later that he had put the baby up for adoption before pumping himself with that ... poison ... until his body gave up on him. It was all such a shame," she ridiculed, shaking her head and reaching for her tea. She took a quick sip and a deep breath. "The one good thing he did was keep the name Mikey and Sarah gave the baby."

Aunt Chi shifted her gaze to Gezie, who was shaking her head slowly in realization of the picture being painted before her. And like the onset of a revelation, Yonna finally understood why they were both called.

"Gezie," Yonna said.

"That's right. After our grandmother, Gizelle Swallowtail."

Before anyone else could react, a quick, audible moan escaped Gezie's mouth. If it weren't for the seriousness of the conversation, someone could have mistaken the sound for a laugh or chuckle. Aunt Chi quickly moved to sit on the couch beside them and took Gezie's hand.

"Nobody, I mean nobody, understood why he did what he did," Aunt Chi comforted, rubbing Gezie's back. "You had family, blood, that wanted you. So, so bad. We have always wanted you."

Gezie let out another sob, then looked up at Aunt Chi. The rest of them—Yonna, Mr. Kwe, and the girls—sat speechless.

"I am so sorry, baby. I should have told you the moment your husband brought you in here for the first time. I knew right away. I would never, could never forget your face. I just—"

Gezie shook her head vigorously. "I ..." she began, stumbling over the words caught in her chest. "Whoooooh." Her exhale was fragile and shaking with emotion. Gathering herself, she closed her eyes and spoke slowly. "I am not crying because I am angry." There it was, this time a clear chuckle between the whimpers of emotion. "I am crying because somehow I knew the whole time."

Gezie turned to face Aunt Chi.

"I knew, Chinara. In my heart of hearts, from that very day. I knew that even if not in this lifetime, we had come across each other before. All those years ..." For a moment, Gezie's emotions broke again and she took another gathering breath. "All those years wondering if I was crazy! I never even told my husband! And now this feels like such a weight lifted off my shoulders."

Gezie turned to Yonna, eyes swollen and red with emotion. "And you, this family did that for you too, didn't they?"

Out of pure instinct, Yonna reached for Gezie's hand and held it between her own two palms as tears flowed from her eyes more than they had in decades. She looked into the eyes of a woman who just a few minutes ago was a stranger, and still somehow understood every way her heart was teetering between the emotions of a world shattering moment, and the emergence of a butterfly from a cocoon. Gezie gazed back, recognizing in Yonna the same thing Yonna recognized in her.

"Wait wait wait," Cleo brashly interrupted. "Let me get this straight. Aunt Chi is Marsha's great-aunt AND your aunt?" she said, pointing at her mother. "So ... that makes Marsha and me ..."

"COUSINS!" the girls squealed simultaneously and laughter lifted the heaviness lingering in the room.

"Yes, little birds. Third cousins to be exact ... but who's counting?" Aunt Chi answered. "How's that for a family tree project?"

The room laughed again, and Gezie wiped away the last of her tears.

Yonna noticed Marsha and Cleo whispering about something where they sat, practically on top of each other in one of the love seats.

"Just tell them! It's the whole reason why we came!" Cleo urged Marsha.

"What y'all over there whispering about? As you can imagine, I've had enough secrets for a lifetime!" Aunt Chi pressed.

Whatever it was, Yonna could tell Marsha was deeply conflicted about sharing.

"Baby, what is it?"

Marsha shook her head as if shaking off any fear and apprehension she felt.

"Ever since the day you told us we were moving, I've been having these dreams, or visions? I'm not really sure how to explain them. In the first one, there was a mockingbird that changed into Uncle VanDyke! And he was talking! Talking and moving just like he did when I was little. He told me I was in a special place called the Traverse, in between the spirit realm and dream realm, where spirits exist as animals after they die. He took me to this huge live oak tree in the middle of a field and told me it was our family tree. When I looked up into it, it was full of swallow-tailed kites. I mean FULL! There had to be dozens of them, and Uncle VanDyke told me each one was one of my ancestors. I wouldn't have believed him if I hadn't already seen him turn into a human from a bird. Then he showed me something else. On the back side of the tree, a huge branch was burning ... and has been burning for a long time. He tried to put the fire out, but he couldn't. He told me I was the only one who could."

Yonna watched her daughter's face closely. Her expressions evolved from wonder, to thrill, to worry. Yonna thought about Marvin and the dream that was troubling him night after night. He had only told her bits and pieces, which was normal while he was trying to figure things out, but she knew that dream was different from how he tossed and turned in their bed whenever it sprang upon him. Aunt Chi and Mr. Kwe looked at each other with a wise concern on each of their faces, silently communicating something in their own marital telepathy. Her gut urged her to listen closer now, for the two were connected in some oracular way.

"Then, I had another one," Marsha continued. "This time Uncle Van-Dyke wasn't there, and the tree was empty, except for a single kite. I tried to talk to it, but it was different from Uncle VanDyke. It didn't turn into a human, but I could tell it was trying to communicate with me. I ... I might have gotten a little frustrated with it, or with the whole situation. I just felt like this whole responsibility to save the family tree was placed on me with no help, no guidance. Then the kite flew off into the woods, and I followed it."

Marsha turned to look at Cleo, with worry in her eyes, as if to ask for help.

"She saw a man being chased by an angry mob!" Cleo inserted, picking up where Marsha left off. "He ran into a cabin, then came back out with a box and a rifle, then disappeared into the woods ahead of the mob. Marsha was hiding, but she could hear the mob searching for the man and smell the smoke from the torches. I can't imagine how scary it must have been," Cleo said, leaning her cheek on Marsha's shoulder.

Then, Cleo looked at her mother, whose expression asked a million and one questions.

"She told me about it when we were researching her ... *our* ... family for the project," Cleo continued. "We found an article that talked about a search party for Michael Cole Swallowtail, and figured it was Marsha's great-grandpa."

Aunt Chi took in a deep breath.

Then, Marsha picked up again.

"As soon as we read the article, the vision of the man running through the woods flashed in my mind. The story in the article seemed off, but I figured it had to be related to my dream somehow. And then we heard you talking about my great-grandpa going missing and ..."

"That's right. Didn't I tell you girls you knew there was something to know?!"

"Hold on," Yonna interjected. "Marsha, why didn't you tell anyone about your dreams?"

"I did! I told Daddy the night I saw the mob! I ran into your room and we both tried to wake you up, but couldn't ... That's when I realized we were both in the Traverse. But it's like he didn't believe that any of it was real. He told me it was just a dream and that reality was more important. So, I figured I would have to do things on my own. Luckily, I met Cleo the next day and ... now we're here."

"Your father wasn't completely wrong, little bird," Aunt Chi explained. "Reality does hold some of the answers, just as you're finding out today. Dreams will guide you to the answers you will find in reality. And the man you saw in your dream was definitely your great-grandfather. I remember that time. We were all scared for him. He told us he was gonna handle it, but that we would likely not see him again. I remember the day we all said goodbye. I knew there was more to the story but we were all too young to hear it. It was grown folks business. I know now that he sacrificed himself to keep us all safe. That is a sad part of our history indeed, but there's pride to be found there as well. What I'm concerned with is this burning tree. Give me a moment, will you all?" Aunt Chi closed her eyes with her palms open in front of her, which made everyone else in the room hold their breath. When she opened her eyes, she shot an inquisitive look at Marsha.

"Tell me more about how you get to the Traverse. Does it happen when you're awake or is it only when you go to sleep?"

Marsha gave Cleo a wide-eyed look before answering.

"I get there by thinking about it before I go to sleep. It's pretty easy to do now that I've been practicing all week. But something strange actually happened this morning. I was waiting for Cleo and there was a kite circling above me. I asked why it was still here and not migrating south for the winter with the rest of the kites. It ignored me, so I closed my eyes and ignored it back." At this, Aunt Chi made a disapproving face.

"Marsha doesn't really like birds much," Yonna explained. "She had a bad experience when she was younger with a sandhill crane."

"I see," Aunt Chi said, then motioned for Marsha to continue.

"When I opened them again the park was gone and the bench was on a trail in the middle of a forest. I heard the bird call and the whole thing disappeared in a moment. I was a little scared, but Cleo calmed me down. It was nothing like what happened in the mob."

"Well, little bird, it's clear to me that you have the gift of clairvoyance. It comes in many different forms, but in your case, you can see into the past. I have something like it, and so do Cleo, Gezie, and your Aunt Marybell. It's why she and I haven't spoken in years, but that's a story for another time. These gifts, which I suspect every Swallowtail has, are a skill that you'll need to master. Yours is strong in you, which is why your uncle was able to get you to the Traverse. It's why he thinks you can put out this fire." Aunt Chi turned to her husband.

"Kwe, this is what the cards have been talking about. The Tower, the Moon, the Ten of Cups."

"I have a gift?" Cleo said, surprised.

"Yes you do, and it seems to be exceptionally strong as well. That's why you're always talking about 'I feel like' and 'something is telling me' … and it's what helped you help Marsha, help us all. It's called claircognizance, and it's the same thing that told your momma she was a part of this family before the words escaped anyone's mouth. Oh boy, we have a lot of work to do here. I don't know why gifts tend to show up in some of us stronger than others, but I know that as we keep solving this mystery, the answers will unfold. Ah!" Aunt Chi gasped and her eyes went as wide as her smile. She got up, quickly rounded the counter and disappeared through the doorway, leaving the fabric fluttering behind her. Mr. Kwe shrugged as if this was completely normal behavior.

When Aunt Chi returned, she was carrying a palm-sized wooden box.

"Lawd, you are doing some GOOD work today! Let me tell you!"

She sat back down next to Mr. Kwe and opened the box. Inside there was an old, golden compass. The chain had been replaced and was several shades brighter than the compass itself, but the compass seemed to be working fine. Aunt Chi held it up and it slowly spun around, revealing a simple engraving on the back side that read *Gizelle*.

"This compass belonged to my grandmother, your great-great-grandmother, the woman who links all of us Swallowtails together. I don't know much of her story, but I know that she speaks to me sometimes. Clairaudience, that's my gift. I can hear things no one else can. She wants you to have this, Marsha. It's going to help you, although I'm sorry to say I don't know how. See, even though I've been working on my gift for years, all I've really gained is control. It's not nearly as strong and clear as the two of yours."

Marsha took the gift and examined the compass face.

"It's beautiful!" she said. "Thank you so much!" She handed it to Cleo. "Do you *feel* anything?"

"Oh, that's not how Cleo's gift works. That's called clairsentience, and I'd ask your Aunt Marybell about that one … or not. She's a little sensitive about it." Aunt Chi laughed at her own joke, but judging from the way Mr. Kwe cleared his throat, it wasn't the most appropriate.

"Hmm," Cleo thought, "I don't feel anything, but I definitely think you should take it with you to bed tonight. And if you can, into the Traverse. That's the thought I had. Is that how it works?" Cleo looked at Aunt Chi.

"Yes, little bird! That's claircognizance for you!"

The family was unpacking the eventful day over the remaining tea when Yonna's phone buzzed in her purse.

"Hello? Wait, wait. Tre. Slow down. What happened? … Oh my, I'm on my way right now!"

"Is everything okay?" Aunt Chi inquired.

"Something's wrong with Marvin. They're at the ER with Dr. Coleman. I … I have to go right now. Gezie, can you—"

"Don't even worry about it. I have the girls. You go!"

"Mommy, what's wrong with Daddy?" Marsha questioned, worry and anxiety filling her eyes.

"I don't know baby, but I'll let you know as soon as I do."

She kissed her daughter and ran out the door.

XI

"Ugggghhhh."

A deep, pounding pain radiated from the back of Marvin's head. He stretched his hand up to rub it out and felt a large lump at the pain's epicenter.

"Wha..?"

Marvin blinked open his eyes and was shocked to find himself propped up against the rough trunk of a tree. The cloudless sky above him was a strange hue of slate blue, and the sun, although it sat in its usual high afternoon position, was dim and filtered, as if a cloud was wrapped around it, absorbing the rays. The clearing looked familiar, but Marvin was too disoriented to decipher where he had seen it before. When he tried to get up to examine more of his surroundings, fatigue pulled him down with a stumble.

"Boy, sit yo' ass down!"

The voice startled Marvin. He looked around, one arm barely stabilizing him on the ground and the other gripping his knee.

"Who's there?" he demanded in a futile attempt to sound intimidating. Instead, his voice came out raspy and weak, confusing and concerning him even more. He had no idea why his body was defying him. He tried to stand once more, this time falling back and bumping his head on the trunk of the tree, sending pain jolting through his temple.

"I said SIT DOWN!" the voice ordered.

Marvin let out a strained moan. Wait. He knew that voice. He knew that voice better than any voice he had known before. But it couldn't be. And if it was ... could that mean ... No. His palms started to sweat again as he looked around, the familiarity growing in tandem with his confusion. There's no way he could be where he thought he was. The last thing he remembered was sitting with Tre in Dr. Coleman's office, very much awake. How did he end up here?

"Boy, calm down before you really find yourself in trouble!"

Yes. There was no mistaking whose voice it was. But where was it coming from? Where *was* he? The outline of a figure appeared in the shadows before him. It carried his own broad shoulders and long face. Marvin squinted his eyes for a better look, just as the figure stepped into the muted sunlight of the strange place.

"Pops?"

And there he was. Michael Cole Swallowtail Jr. Mikey. His father. Alive. And here with him.

"Hey, son. You're in pretty bad shape."

Marvin couldn't believe it. It had been over a decade since his father's funeral. He rubbed his forehead, trying to make sense of what he was seeing before him.

"Am ... am I dead?"

"You ain't dead, boy. But you gon' be if you don't pull yourself togeth-er soon. You and your brother. Who would have thought your mother and I put all of that time into raising y'all just for y'all to turn out to be nothing but stubborn and hard headed? You should be ashamed of your-selves. Now, I know your brother has been asking a lot of you lately and you have every right to feel how you feel. And I'm not gon' sit here and act like I didn't have a role to play in that. There are a lot of things, son, that you just don't understand. And that's on me too. But the way you treated your brother today, the things you did to try and make him feel how you feel, I have no words for that. That's not the Marvin I know, nor the son your mother and I raised."

At this point, confused couldn't describe even half of what Marvin was feeling.

"Pops, I don't know what you're talking about. Is this a dream or something? Where am I?"

"Come on, son!" Mikey replied in his sing-songy frustration. "I know you hit your head pretty hard in that fall, but pull yourself together! You were in your boy Derrick's office. He told you Tre would need a trans-plant. You, bottling your feelings up like you always do, got so anxious that your body faked a heart attack. Or something like that. I can't re-member everything the doctor said. When you tried to get up and leave, your body gave out and you hit your head."

It all started to come back to Marvin. Dr. Coleman's assessment, the feeling in his chest, Tre's words. He clenched his jaw and adjusted himself on the ground.

"So why am I here and not in the hospital?"

"You are in the hospital. Your body at least. Your mind is here."

"Where is *here*, Pops? You're not telling me nothing!"

"Oh, don't give me that. You know exactly where *here* is. You've been coming here since you were a little boy. The same place you saw Tre begging for his life. The same place you saw your mother and me when ours were coming to an end. The same place your daughter found you the other day—and oh, by the way, you completely ignored all the things she was trying to tell you. You have a special one on your hands and it's a damn shame how you don't even see it. "

Marvin looked away from his father, not wanting to let the words take root in his heart. But the man told no lies. Marvin did know this place, he just wished to God that he didn't. Nothing came from here but death for him, and he wanted to protect Marsha from the visions this place had brought him in his childhood.

"Like I've been saying. You might not be dead yet, but with each stupid, stubborn decision you've been making, you just keep digging your grave deeper and deeper."

"Me?! What about your other son? He's the one who's been killing himself for years! Everyone's always getting on me about how I react to it. How about we look at the root of the problem? Tre got himself into this. Tre got everyone into this! I'm the one who always has his back. Who always has to clean up his mess. And what the hell does he do other than step all over it again? If my grave is being dug, Tre's the one who's digging it. Not me!"

Marvin didn't care about his physical pain anymore. The hurt in his heart trumped everything his body was feeling. He sat there on the ground, staring up at his father like a little boy throwing a temper tantrum. But he did not care. He had to get this off of his chest. Marvin glared at the old man, breathing hard through his anger, and the thought occurred to him that maybe he was targeting the wrong person all along. He smiled at this and let out a chuckle.

"You know what? Maybe Tre isn't the problem. Maybe the blame falls on you! You always let him get away with things. Even up until the day you died. You gave him chance after chance. But let me make one mistake, and you were on my ass like the bark on this tree!"

"Watch yourself now," Mikey threatened.

"No! I tried to do everything right. I made up for everything he lacked, and you never saw it! You never saw me! Your head was too far up his—"

"Marvin Cole Swallowtail, I swear, if you say one more word outta line I will rise from the dead and snatch you down here with me!" Mikey took a step closer and pointed at his son, jaw quivering with anger.

"Ahh, there it is," Marvin resolved. "Why don't you just say it plain? You never wanted a second son, even if we were twins. It was clear when you named him Michael and me Marvin. I guess the joke *is* on me then. Spending so much of my time and energy trying to make you proud, make you see what he really is ... Nothing I could have done or will do is good enough. Man, I don't need this shit. I have a family of my own. A wife who sees me and loves me better than y'all ever could. Forget all this. I don't need none of it!"

Marvin pulled himself up from the ground and braced himself on the tree. When he looked back at his father he saw something he never had before. Mikey was still glaring, but in the inner corner of his eyes something shimmered in the faint light of the Traverse. They stood there for a long moment while solitary tears dropped, one by one, down the outline of the Swallowtail nose. Marvin tilted his chin away, trying to mask the tears forming in his own eyes. With no fight left in him, he sank back to the ground, defeated. When Marvin raised his eyes to face his father, something in the man's expression had changed as well. The anger had subsided and was replaced by ... was it concern? No. It was something else.

"I'm sorry, son."

"What?" Marvin retorted, face twisted into an ugly mix of surprise, anger, and shock.

"I said I am sorry." Mikey let out a deep sigh. "The last thing I came here to do is argue with you. I am to blame here. None of it falls on you, son. The blame is all on me. And I ... I am sorry."

Marvin's breath was heavy and staccatoed under his tears. He shook his head, trying his best to resist the effect of the words he had always wanted, needed to hear. From anyone, everyone. Especially his father.

"I'm sorry for not letting you know how proud I was, am ... have *always* been of you. I'm sorry for not holding your brother accountable for the ways he hurt us all, and more importantly, himself. But most of all, I'm sorry for not letting you know the parts of me that I regretted the most. The parts that made me human, that showed how far from perfect I truly was. Maybe then the two of you wouldn't have fallen into the same curses as Lil' Marv and me. I thought I was doing what was best for both of you. Loving y'all how you needed to be loved. But I see now what a grave mistake I made. I didn't just pull your name out of nowhere. I named you after the most important man in my life aside from my own father. I tried my hardest to treat you better than I treated him. But I see now how I failed."

Marvin couldn't look at his father, not with the tears that were now flowing uncontrollably. With each word, the tangled knot in Marvin's stoic heart was unraveling. Unable to speak himself, Marvin dropped his head and could do nothing else but listen.

"My baby cousin, Marvin—we all called him Lil' Marv. A lot of people know him for the tragic way his life ended, but not many people knew the way he lived, like I did. I remember the day he was born. I was five or six years old, it was just after my daddy disappeared. I was excited, you see, because everyone kept telling me what a responsibility I was going to have when Lil' Marv got there. My little self felt like I was gonna be a daddy or something. I was so mad that I couldn't go to the hospital with my mom ... Ha." Mikey wiped the tears away from his face. "When they finally brought him home, I didn't know how to act! I feel like I spent the next three years waiting for him to be big enough to actually play with him. You know, back then, all of us, Marybell, Chinara, Lil' Marv, we were all as close as could be. It was like that our whole childhood. And Lil' Marv, no one could tell me that wasn't my little brother. I tried to teach him right from wrong, and how to be a man. He was funny, had the biggest heart, and he was smart! Man, was that boy smart!" Mikey laughed to himself. "It used to make me mad. I guess I thought since I was older I oughta be smarter, but he outwitted me any chance he got!"

"Things changed when I went away to school and then off to war ... I got caught up in my own life. I didn't ... I wasn't there for him during his most pivotal years. By the time I got back, he had gone astray. My own experiences made it hard for me to relate to him. Instead of being there for Lil' Marv, I ridiculed him, critiqued him. And yeah, he did some pretty messed up things but," Mikey shook his head in shame, "all he needed was somebody to be there for him. I couldn't find it in my heart to forgive him for some of the things he did. I never got over my guilt after he died. And I tried to make up for it in the way I raised y'all. But the truth is, when I looked into Tre's eyes, even as a little boy, I saw the same thing that sent Lil' Marv astray. And son, when I look into yours right now, I see the grudge that sent me to my grave." Mikey shook his head vigorously. "I refuse to let you suffer the same fate as me."

Mikey took a seat on the ground next to his son and rested his wrists on his knees.

"I thought if I pushed you to be the man I couldn't be for Lil' Marv, and gave Tre the love I couldn't give him, neither of you would make the same mistakes I did. But you two are your own people. Your own men. And that resentment you carry in your heart, I know it all too well. It will kill you if you let it. Yeah, your past is on me, rightfully so. But your present and your future, Marvin, that's on you, son."

Marvin used the back of his hand to wipe the heavy tears from his face and raised his head to his father. Through bloodshot eyes, he could see Mikey's sincerity. His unease. His care.

"If I'm being real, Pops, it's not even Tre that I'm mad at," Marvin finally admitted. "And it's definitely not you. You and Mom did a great job. I'm mad at myself because, you know, I don't want to be resentful. But I don't know how to be there for him without that happening. I need something back from him. I need to see that, if I give him my liver, if I give him life, he's not gonna waste it."

"I understand that, but that's not your call, and it doesn't fall on your shoulders," Mikey said. "Tre is going to do what he is going to do. And his cancer is a testimony that he's gonna have to live with his decisions. My question to you is, what can you do to ensure that you can live with yourself? Not out of duty, or responsibility, because those things only go so far. But really live with yourself and be proud of the man you are, outside of what anyone else has to say?"

Mikey stood and pulled Marvin up with him. Propping one arm over his neck, he helped his son walk out into the clearing until the whole tree was visible. Marvin thought back to his childhood, before his visions of death tainted his dreams with fear and apprehension. Back then, this clearing, this tree was his escape. He'd spend his boyish dreamtime playing in its branches, nibbling on the cranberry, hibiscus, and blackberry brambles growing in patches where the dim sun broke through. It had been so long since he had traveled here, and in that moment, he realized his resentful instincts stretched much further than people who hurt him. He had built resentment towards this place too. This place that showed him deaths that he was not prepared for, called him to be a man he wasn't ready to be. But he had forgotten that it had also held him when the real world squeezed him out of places he thought he belonged in. Middle school breakups, high school insecurities, college rejections, it was here he fled to. Resting his thoughts in the deep wrinkles of the oak's bark reminded him that beneath the protective roughness, his life's challenges brought highways of nourishment, sweet saps, and strong foundations. After seeing his parents' deaths, he blamed this tree, instead of seeing the ways the visions were meant to uplift and protect him. But it was time for him to forgive. Not just the tree. Not just Tre. It was time for him to forgive himself.

"You see that?" Mikey said, pointing at a large branch towards the back of the tree. Until then, Marvin hadn't noticed the smoldering branch.

"That right there is what happens to us when we let guilt, resentment, anger, sorrow—anything like that fester in our family. It's what happens when we get too far away from each other to remember what family means in the first place. We've been split for so long, I don't know what this tree looks like any other way. But I do know us Swallowtails, we are a strong, special people. And when we are united, no fire could ever truly burn us. Help us get there, son. You and that special little girl of yours. Please. Before it all falls down. "

MARSHA WATCHED THE TREES PASS THROUGH THE WINDOW of Gezie's car. It was only a short ride from Aunt Chi's to her house, but it felt like hours passed while her head struggled to wrap itself around the day's events. As soon as her thoughts settled on one thing, the nuances and emotions around the thought came flooding in, sending her mind spinning in circles like a top. At the news of her father, her day had gone from terrific to tumultuous in a matter of seconds. What could possibly be wrong with him? He was perfectly fine just that morning! Yeah, maybe he was a little stressed, but there was no sign of him being sick! And sick enough to be in the hospital? That sounded crazy.

"Hey, Marsha, we're here sweetie," Gezie said, tenderly looking through the rearview mirror.

"You okay?" Cleo asked softly, reaching for Marsha's hand. This gentle touch eased some of Marsha's angst, and the realization set in that in the past week, Cleo had not only become Marsha's closest friend, but her cousin. Marsha had a cousin! A person her age, who knew her and liked her for who she was. Their shared history affected them both, and now, the burden of putting out their family fire didn't seem like Marsha's to bear alone. It was this thought which kept Marsha from spiraling over concerns about her father.

"Mrs. Gezie, does Cleo have to go home right now?" Marsha finally said, looking towards the front seat of the car.

"Of course not. Cleo, call me when you're ready, and keep me posted, okay?"

"Okay! I will," Cleo assured.

"And Marsha, you don't have to call me Mrs. if you don't want to. We're family now. You can call me Auntie."

The girls exited the vehicle and headed towards the front of Marsha's house.

"Are you ready to meet my siblings?" Marsha asked in a warning tone while knocking on the door.

Cleo replied with a bright smile. It didn't take much to notice her attempts to keep Marsha's spirits high, which Marsha appreciated more than she could show.

"Who is it?" Jeremy teased from inside.

"It's me! Can you open up? It's hot out here!"

"Who is me?"

"Marsha! Your sister!" She yelled as her patience ran thin.

"My sister is inside already. Who are you, you imposter?! I should call the police."

Marsha kissed her teeth.

"Jeremy, I'm really not in the mood for this! And I have company! Open the dooooor!"

Cleo giggled at Marsha.

"Yeah, it's funny now but this is your new cousin. It's only a matter of time before he unleashes his terror on you."

There was some murmuring from inside the house and a few moments later the door opened, and Marissa let the girls inside.

A few hours later Yonna called Marissa to let the children know they would be home soon. Marsha was finally able to relax, so Cleo called her mother and headed home. The girls had decided to wait until their project was complete to tell the rest of the family who Cleo really was.

Marsha was working on placing the new names to her family tree when she saw two familiar cars pull into the driveway: her dad's black Cadillac and Uncle Tre's old Chevy pickup. By the time she made it downstairs, her mother was working to unlock the door, but Marsha opened it while the key was still in the lock. Her eyes immediately set on her uncle and father, who had one arm draped over his brother's shoulder. It was a matter of seconds before Marissa and Jacob were at the door too. Normally, under these sorts of circumstances their parents would be bombarded with questions—*Daddy, are you okay? Mommy, what happened? Daddy, what do you need?* But something about the image of their father, the man who typically held their world on his shoulders, being held up by someone else, kept the children silent and focused on letting them slowly make their way inside. Even Jacob held back his usual rambunctious greeting and "helped" Uncle Tre and Yonna get their father settled on the couch. Once he was, Yonna went to the kitchen to prepare some food for them all.

Marsha sat on the floor in front of the bookshelf and studied the adults, their faces and actions, trying to understand the origin of the mood. Her mother was quite tense, and moved through the kitchen carefully, periodically stopping to take a few deep breaths. Uncle Tre's body language was interesting and hard to read. He couldn't decide between a seat on their La-Z-Boy adjacent to the couch, or standing by the large center island that separated the kitchen and living room. Either way, even though he kept his distance, his mind was clearly focused on his brother, anxiously glancing over at him every few seconds. It seemed like he was deeply concerned and wanted to help, but didn't know how to. Marsha shifted her attention back to her father, whom she noted looked surprisingly calm and peaceful. Maybe Mom got it wrong? Maybe Uncle Tre was the one in the hospital? Marsha quickly lost hope in that thought, remembering how her father leaned on her uncle when they first arrived at the door. That was strange, too. The many questions sent Marsha's head spinning again.

Perhaps sensing Marsha approaching her brink, Marvin broke the wordlessness.

"I appreciate y'all letting us get settled before you start throwing questions at us."

"Of course, Daddy," Marissa said, walking back from the kitchen with a glass of water.

"So ..." Marsha dragged out the word to make it clear she was expecting some answers.

"I wanna talk to everyone at the same time. Where's your brother?"

"Don't be mad, he hasn't even told me yet," Yonna said with a harmless annoyance in her voice.

Marsha hadn't even noticed Jeremy didn't come down when their parents arrived. Her mother yelled his name, and as soon as she heard him stomping down the stairs, Marsha's mouth went dry. Somehow she knew something was about to erupt, and she tried hard to fight her urge to leave the room. She needed her questions answered, so she stayed put.

A few moments later, Jeremy rounded the corner. He immediately saw his father resting on the couch, a large bandage on the back of his head.

"Damn, what the hell happened to you?"

"Jeremy!"

"Excuse me?"

"Boy, have you lost your mind?"

Marissa, Yonna, and Uncle Tre all spoke at the same time, echoing the shock of Jeremy's audacity.

Marvin didn't even look up. Instead, an edged smile crept across his face. Now Marsha was completely perplexed. She thought back to the weekend before when she caught her father glaring at Jeremy just moments before he asked her about his language. Now, it was as if her dad and Uncle Tre had switched personalities. She looked nervously at Marissa, then at her mother, and finally Uncle Tre, whose anger still flickered in his eyes like fire. Eyes fixed on Jeremy.

"What?" Jeremy doubled down. "I'm supposed to be all worried just because he busted his ass?"

In a split second Uncle Tre was across the room with his fists full of Jeremy's T-shirt, pinning him to the wall. Marissa screamed at the impact and Jacob ran to their mother, wailing in fear. Jeremy's fists were balled and his face maintained its rage, but Marsha saw the fear flash in his eyes.

"Let him go!" Marvin said loud and firm. He didn't yell, but the volume of command in his tone hung in the air, suspending the moment. Tre and Jeremy stayed locked in their stare down, forcing out audible breaths until finally, Jeremy gave in and looked away. The only sounds left were Yonna's coos, attempting to calm the baby.

"Let him go," Marvin commanded again but this time with a calm that might have scared Marsha if she was on the receiving end.

"If he wants to talk with the men, then let him."

Marvin turned, sharpened his gaze, and looked Jeremy in the eye.

"But if you wanna talk with the men, you better learn how to talk like a man. And that means respect comes first. If you have something to say, say it, but you better watch your tongue."

Uncle Tre finally let go of his grip, and Jeremy stood like a bull preparing to charge, gaining his composure. Marvin nodded at the couch and Jeremy moved to take a seat, albeit as far away from his father as possible. He made sure not to lock eyes with him. Marsha never saw her brother like this before. Where was the amusement he usually kept during his rampages? The smile and laugh that came the moment he knew he got to you? Instead, every expression on his face was of rage, pain, and frustration. Composing himself, Uncle Tre stood behind the couch and folded his arms across his chest. Marvin hadn't even stood up. He took a sip of water then nodded at his son to speak.

Jeremy visibly struggled to keep his voice steady.

"Why would I trust anything you have to say about being a man, when you broke the main rule you taught me about it?" Jeremy finally looked up at his father, jaw clenched, breath getting deeper with each word he spoke.

"Don't just tell the truth, be the truth. And stand on it. Because at least if you do that much, you can live with yourself knowing that you have. That's what you said. So, tell me, how do you sleep at night? Knowing that you took your kids away from their real family, just to snatch us from the one we built ourselves? And knowing that you lied about it to save your own—"

"Boy!" Marvin cut him off and shot a look that issued a final warning.

"And lied about it for your own benefit," Jeremy corrected himself.

XII

Marvin slowly turned to face the rest of his family.

"Is this how all of you feel?"

Marsha was taken aback. For once, there was a reason behind Jeremy's behavior. A reason that Marsha actually agreed with. And the silence across the room spoke volumes. Marsha watched her father curiously. Marvin's expression softened more, and he let out the air in his chest, dropping his shoulders just the slightest bit.

He wiped his hand over his mouth as if gathering the words he didn't want to let slip out. He nodded a few times to some unknown resolution in his mind and looked at his son again.

"Being a man ain't always about what you do. Sometimes, it's about how you respond to what you've done. Sometimes you gotta take risks, and you won't always know the outcome—the hurt your actions might cause, or the truths they might reveal. It's what you do in those moments—that's how you define your truth. You can make it all about yourself, or you can take accountability for how your decisions—good or bad—might have affected everyone around you, and how you respond to it all."

He turned to face the room.

"Jeremy is not wrong to be upset at me. None of you are. I lied, and that was a mistake. And what happened to me today was my wake up call. My mind and body turned against me. And it wasn't because of the anger or frustration. It was the guilt, and the effect that trying to hold it all in had on me. I didn't know this was how things would turn out when I made the decision to move back to Ocala. I thought that if I made sure you all had what you needed—a home, a spot on the football team—then that would be enough." Addressing Jeremy directly, Marvin continued, "Perhaps, when you are a father, you will realize that things aren't so black and white all the time. But I hope it doesn't take you as long as it took me.

I hope you realize sooner rather than later that taking your emotions out on me, or your siblings, only ends up hurting you."

Marvin let out a growl as he sat up through his pain.

"I am sorry for lying to you. For uprooting your lives to try to fix the mistakes I've made in my own, and being blind to your true needs afterwards. I'm sorry to my wife for the ways my stubbornness has put you in countless impossible situations that somehow, by the grace of God, you help me work out. And to my brother—"

"Don't," Tre stopped him. "This ain't about me right now."

Marvin nodded and turned back to face Jeremy.

"Son, I'm sorry for not being the man I'm trying to raise you to be. I'm sorry for folding on you. You asked me how I sleep at night? I sleep knowing that I'm the type of father who will allow himself to be an example if it means his children will be better versions of him. That they don't have to learn the same lessons the hard way. So *you* tell *me*, Jeremy Cole, is what I'm doing right now enough to show you that? To demonstrate how to be bold enough to not only take risks, but to apologize for them, in word and in action?"

Jeremy's mouth quivered and pinched the air as he failed to hold back his tears. On the other side of the room, Jacob squirmed free of his mother's arms and ran to the couch, stopping just before the father and son. Then he hugged them, first grabbing Jeremy's leg then reaching over to loop his little fingers around his father's. Jeremy looked back up at his father, and quickly found himself in an embrace. Jacob crawled up into the space between them and wrapped his arms around their necks. Marissa folded herself over them from behind the couch and Marsha, tears streaming down her face, crawled across the carpet and joined the group hug.

Later that night, after dinner dishes were complete and the children had withdrawn to their rooms for the night, Yonna found Marvin sitting in bed reading *The Obsidian*, the book he promised Marsha he would read the day they met the children at Aunt Marybell's house.

"Is it as good as she said it was?"

"Absolutely! Our girl's got great taste." Marvin folded down the corner of the page he was reading to close the book and give his wife his full attention.

Yonna leaned in the threshold between their bedroom and bathroom.

"You know, I'm really proud of you. I can't say I was expecting that."

"Yeah, it's been quite a day. I had this ... revelation at the hospital before I woke up."

"Oh, yeah? What happened?"

"I don't know if I ever told you this, but when I was a little boy I used to dream a lot."

"Used to?"

The couple chuckled and Yonna went to take a seat next to him on their bed.

"Well, I guess I still do but ... it was different back then. I would go to this place ..."

"The Traverse?"

Marvin looked at his wife surprised.

"Yeah ... how'd you know?"

"Marsha and I have had quite the day ourselves. But we can talk about that later."

"Ahh. Yeah, I still gotta talk to Marsha ... I really fumbled that one. I didn't call it the Traverse back then, but loved that place when I was her age. It was where I would go to escape. When I got older and I met you, I didn't need to escape as much, so it just became something like a second home when I was asleep. Something void of all of my daily stresses and responsibilities. It was my safe space. Until it wasn't. I ... I've never told anyone this part before."

Marvin took a deep breath in, and released it slowly.

"I saw my parents die there. Both of them. In a vision, just a few weeks before they died in real life."

Marvin spoke so plainly and calmly, as if he was telling a story about his football career, not recalling the most terrible moments of his life. But that was his way, and although Yonna's heart sank, she held her composure, solidifying the safe space for him to speak freely. She reached for his hand, which he squeezed before continuing.

"At first I was so confused, I didn't know how to react. I felt betrayed by it. Even as a grown man, something in me broke and I wanted nothing to do with the Traverse anymore. But sometimes it's out of my control. And that's why when we were in Key West and Tre called ... I knew we had to do something."

"When did you see him? When was the dream?" Yonna asked gently as she put the pieces together in her own mind.

"The night before he called," he shook his head, remembering. "I tried to save him! But this time the vision kept happening over and over ... and after a while ... I got tired. I guess I wanted to see what would happen if I didn't save him. That night, when I let Tre go, I woke up to Marsha in the Traverse with me. I panicked. I didn't want her to have to go through the same things I was going through, or experience the same heartbreak I did when the Traverse showed me more than what I was prepared to know."

Yonna listened with every part of her being. It had been so long since Marvin opened up like this. He was by no means closed off to her—they lived a happy life and shared a timeless bond. But continuing to learn about each other after two decades was something truly special. That's what this whole situation had brought to them, she resolved to herself. She learned more about the man she loved, but more importantly, she was learning about herself. Hearing her husband admit his guilt in such a secure and confident way created space for her to address her own.

"Today when I was still unconscious, I saw my dad. And he apologized. And now I wonder, if I had just let go of my fear for one second, maybe we could have had the conversation we had today, back then, and it could have saved him. But either way, when it comes to this family, I can't leave that to chance."

"You know you weren't the only one to blame here," Yonna finally admitted. "And I think I've been walking around carrying a lot of guilt as well. I didn't speak up when I knew you were making the wrong decision. I kind of let you take the fall, and I am so, so sorry. I'm supposed to be your teammate. Your council. But I just watched."

"Oh baby, you have absolutely nothing to apologize for. I had already made up my mind. And while yes, you are my teammate and my most trusted council, I needed to go through this. I needed to make this mistake, and most importantly, I needed to overcome it. I needed my children to see me. And if it makes you feel better, you may not have said anything with your words, but your expressions said a whole lot. This ain't our first time at the party," he joked, smiling at her.

Yonna couldn't help but smile back. She wiped the tears from her eyes and tilted her forehead to meet his.

"I know you," Marvin said softly. "I know you disapproved. At the end of the day it was my decision. And you, you are my rock through it all. And like I said earlier, I just need to stop putting you in hard places."

"That's only gon' happen when you stop testing out how hard your head can be." Yonna slowly turned his head to each side and examined the bandages. "You really took a tumble, didn't you."

The pair laughed and sank deeper into their embrace while Yonna told Marvin all about her day with Aunt Chi. Before too long, they fell asleep wrapped in each other's arms.

XIII

MARSHA SAT ALONE BY HER FAMILY TREE. The kite that had been following her was not there, and she wondered if she had finally gone too far by telling it to leave earlier that day. Maybe it had actually left and flown south for the winter. Just as she considered this, she heard footsteps approaching. When she looked, she was surprised to see her father standing there in the glow of the Traverse moon.

"Hey, baby girl," he said, with a soft, gentle smile.

"Daddy!" Marsha jumped to her feet and readied an excuse as to why she was disobeying her father's order to stay away from the Traverse. "I'm sorry, I can explain!"

"Don't worry, baby. It's all good. I actually owe you an apology for that too." Marvin chuckled at the irony of this, being that just a few hours before, his father was apologizing to him under the same tree. Marvin nodded his head towards the trunk, inviting Marsha to sit with him. It was silent for a moment as they both sat connected to the tree in their own way.

"You know, I used to come here a lot when I was your age," Marvin began.

"Really?" Marsha said, trying to picture her father as a young boy.

"Yup, I sure did. I'd come to think, hang out with the birds. Just get away from things, you know?"

"Yeah. I do. It can be really peaceful here."

There was another pause as a short breeze blew through the tree's branches, shaking the leaves in a calm chorus.

"Why'd you stop?" Marsha asked when the breeze passed.

Marvin stroked his beard, gathering his thoughts before answering.

"I started having some strange visions. Scary visions. But unlike you, I wasn't brave enough to figure out what they were trying to tell me before it was too late."

Marsha flashed a proud smile, reveling in the thought of being more brave than her father, and Marvin nudged her with his elbow.

"I still haven't figured it out yet either," Marsha admitted. "I mean, yeah we've discovered a lot and a lot is happening, but ... the branch is still burning."

"So tell me what you know so far. Maybe we can put this fire out together."

"Okay, I know that the fire got bigger when Uncle Tre got sick. Uncle VanDyke told me that. But no one knows when it started burning in the first place. I know that ever since I started having the dreams, I started meeting more of our family. And with each clue I get from the dreams, I get some sort of corresponding clue in real life. I know that the man I saw running from the mob was your grandfather. None of this made the fire smaller." Marsha shook her head at this, then looked to her father and asked him the same question he had asked her.

"Well, I know that Tre's sickness got worse when I got closer, but that's because of the feelings I had towards him. So the way we love each other definitely affects the fire. But clearly, forgiveness alone doesn't put it out," Marvin said.

Marsha thought deeply about everything they had discovered in the past week. It still wasn't adding up. There were still too many holes in the story.

"Maybe we need to go back further than just you and Uncle Tre. Maybe we need to go back to the last time everyone was together. Before Great-Grandpa Swallowtail disappeared."

Marsha reached into her pocket, feeling for the compass she received earlier that day. She pulled it out and held it up for Marvin to see. It spun softly in the moonlight, flashing its face like a traveler's star.

"Aunt Chi gave me this today. She said something told her it would be useful. It belonged to her grandmother, Michael Sr.'s mother, Gizelle Swallowtail."

"Huh, that's strange," Marvin noted, examining the relic. "Our house should be north of here, but this doesn't point that way."

Marsha took the compass in her hand and twisted it from side to side, tracking the needle head.

"It points to the tree!" Marsha and Marvin looked at each other with the same expression of intrigue and perplexity.

Just then, a swallow-tailed kite screeched its loud, piercing call and came into view. It flew around the tree once, twice, and then on the third time, disappeared into the branches. A moment later, there was a blur of light and a woman rounded the base of the tree. She was old and rather short, but carried a mighty presence with her. Her gray-white hair was parted in the center into two long braids draping over each shoulder. Her horizontal patchwork skirt was floor-length and full, with every color you could imagine laid on top of a white underskirt. She wore a cropped white poncho made of thin, loose-knitted fabric and shells stitched into the trimming over a plain white cotton blouse. Her wrinkled skin was adorned with beaded jewelry around her neck, hair, and wrists. Everything about her fashion looked Native, but her features boasted strong and prominent West-African descent. The woman yawned and stretched her arms out wide as she walked towards them, as if she was waking up from a long nap.

Marvin and Marsha rose from their seated position, and Marvin stepped in front of his daughter in defense.

"Ahhh," the old woman groaned. "Decades trapped in bird form really does a number on the joints."

"Oh, well hello there!" she chirped, finally noticing Marvin. "I'm looking for a girl named Marsha. Have you seen her?"

"I'm Marsha's father … who are you?"

"Who … Who am I? I am Gizelle Swallowtail, Marsha's great-great-grandmother. Oh this thing sho' is starting to make sense now. Marsha's father … so that must make you … let me think, let me think … Oh, that's right. Marvin! Hmph. Marvin." Gizelle cut him a side-eyed glance, then a big, warm smile slipped across her face. "You look so much like them all." She had a nostalgic glimmer in her eye as she spoke about the Swallowtail men. "And where is little Miss Marsha Claire?"

"I … I'm here. I'm Marsha." She stepped out from her hiding place and revealed herself.

"Of course you are. It is such a pleasure to finally meet you. I have been trying to get your attention for days."

The pieces clicked in Marsha's head. The kite that led her to the tree a week ago, the one that flew above her during the daytime vision, they were all the same bird! They were all this woman—Gizelle Swallowtail.

"That was you, wasn't it? The bird that kept popping up anywhere I went?"

"It sho' was. I've been following you since your uncle told you about this here tree. But I couldn't assume my human form until you had something physical of mine to tether me to it. That's why I whispered to your Aunt Chi to give you that compass. Now, I wasn't expecting to run into your father too, but I am glad I did."

"That was you too?"

"Yes, it was. I assume y'all know by now about the burning branch?" Gizelle tilted her head down as if she were glancing at them over invisible glasses.

Just then, the fire cracked and sent embers flying high into the sky. Marvin pulled Marsha towards him and covered her head with his own. Gizelle ducked her head down as best as her aged body would let her.

"Yeah, we know about it," Marvin said uneasily, slowly rising to let Marsha go.

"Do you know how to put it out?" Marsha asked, confused as to why the woman had no sense of urgency even after the mini explosion.

"Put it out? There ain't no way to put that fire out. I'm sorry to tell ya, but that branch gon' burn."

"What?" Marsha was mortified. She looked at her father, tears swelling in her eyes. He was just as concerned. All of the searching she had done, all of the dreams, arguments, and tears ... it was all for nothing if she couldn't put that fire out.

"Oh baby girl, it's alright! That branch needs to burn. As a matter of fact, it already has! But that tree, that tree is strong, and all we need to worry about is keeping it that way. Y'all two come with me now, I'll explain it all."

Gizelle started walking away from the tree. Marvin grabbed his daughter's hand, gave her a reassuring look, then led her after the woman and away from the tree.

"I thought I made it clear to my children to make sure all of the descendants knew our story!" Gizelle complained, waddling through the low brush of the clearing. "I see that they dropped the ball there. I'm surprised y'all are even here, being that your gifts are only supposed to work under that pretense ..."

"Gifts? Like the ones Aunt Chi was talking about?" Marsha questioned.

"That's right! You're a smart one, aren't ya?" Gizelle winked at Marsha. "You all have them. Each one of my descendants. You two can see me, so you must have gotten the gift of sight. Some of y'all, like Chinara, can hear, some can feel, and some just know things. The knowing things one is strong in Cleo. Be sure you thank her after all of this is said and done. Lord knows the trouble I had to go through to make sure y'all ended up in the same class."

Of course she did that too.

"Wow. So you really set this whole thing up," Marsha concluded, somewhat fascinated and inspired by the woman's intricate plot.

"Of course I did! Like Cleo taught you, my job as your ancestor is to support and guide you all for your own good, and the good of our lineage as a whole. The thing is, it's a big job to do alone. And because of the generational mess that has been accumulating, I've had to do it alone for far too long." Gizelle stopped and looked at her descendants. "I'm getting tired, you hear me? Now I could sit and try to point a finger, find someone to blame, but Marvin, as I know you recently discovered, we all had a hand to play in this."

Marvin nodded in agreement.

"What about the gifts? Were the gifts a part of your plan too?"

"Mmhm. But let's not get too far ahead of ourselves. It's important to understand the why before you learn too much of the what."

Gizelle guided them towards the trailhead where Marsha had seen her great-grandfather just a week ago.

Marsha stopped just before entering.

"I don't want to go in there. Last time I did ..."

Gizelle stopped and turned to face the child. She had a frustrated look on her face, but when she saw Marsha's worry, she softened and walked to stand just before her. Marsha looked into her great-great-grandmother's eyes and saw her own. There was a ferocity, a resilience, but also a deep, penetrating concern. Gizelle gently placed her palm on Marsha's cheek.

"I should not have shown you that alone." Gizelle looked at Marvin apologetically. "That was a lapse in judgment on my part. But you all need to know our history in order to truly understand why all of this is happening. Your father can tell you. Although they seem real, these are just visions. Nothing can hurt you here, ain't that right Marvin?"

Marvin paused before answering, remembering all he had been through in this place, then nodded his head in agreement.

"First of all, I'm here with you this time," he assured his daughter, "and I got you no matter what. But secondly, you're not new to this baby. You know if things get to be too much, you're still in control, just like you were that night. You just close your eyes and will yourself back to safety, and you'll find yourself there."

Marsha took a deep breath. Her father had a point. She had gotten out of a scary situation alone already, and this time she was with her father and her great-great-grandmother, who clearly had powers beyond Marsha's understanding. She was scared, but she desperately wanted to learn how to help her family. If Marsha couldn't do anything about the fire, the least she could do was this, whatever it was.

"Okay, let's do it," she said. With this, Gizelle grabbed Marsha's hand and continued into the forest with Marvin protectively following behind.

"It's not that far from here," the old woman said, "just around this bend."

A few steps later, the trail broke into a small clearing with a tiny cabin sitting in the middle.

"This is the cabin I saw that night!" Marsha whispered.

"Yes, it sho' is. This is the cabin my husband and I raised the first generation of Swallowtails in. Michael, Winona, Millie and Lanae were all born right here in this cabin. Come, let's sit so I can rest my feet. I have quite the story to show you both."

Marsha sat between Marvin and Gizelle on the steps of the cabin. Gizelle placed her hands on her thighs, palms facing up, and closed her eyes. Marsha noticed a ripple in the forest before her and squinted for a better look.

"I was born into slavery way back when," Gizelle began. "I lived on a plantation in South Carolina growing rice. My mother was stolen from West Africa, and my father from somewhere in the Caribbean. They were both powerful, magical people." As Gizelle spoke, the forest scenery before them started to shift and match the visions that Gizelle was crafting. Projected in front of them was a baby held in the massive hands of its father, and a mother proudly gazing down over the man's shoulder.

"Like me, my mother was a storyteller and passed down our histories through the lessons and tales that she wove. My father was a warrior, so he didn't last long on the plantation. After his death, my mother and some other leaders staged a revolt."

The forest before them turned to a small, dimly lit room with several faces conspiring together to craft a plan. At the center, the face of the mother, hardened by time and loss, focused on revenge and justice.

"It was successful until it wasn't," Gizelle explained, "and then I lost her too. I guess they figured I'd be as disruptive as my parents were, so I was moved into the house and, well, let's just say I wouldn't wish that on any young girl."

Marsha saw a young girl being led by a white man into a room on the second floor of an old colonial style mansion. She didn't want to think about what happened on the other side of that door. She was relieved when the scene shifted again to the same girl, now a young woman, hiding in the dark depths of a swamp with a few other people.

"When I was about twenty or so, rumors started to spread about freedoms that could be found in Florida—instead of trying to work your way into the railroad, if you ran south, you might have better luck. I had learned a lot from my mama and so I called on the spirits to help me, and the first chance I got, I escaped. It was that blessing which got me here."

In the forest theater before Marsha, the group followed the coastal swamps south by night, and then climbed into trees to hide during the day.

"It was a long, terrifying journey. Along the way, we ran into some communities of escaped slaves. They were so well hidden that if you didn't know to look, there was no way you'd ever realize they were there. Some of the people I traveled with wanted to stay, and for me to stay with them. But I knew that wasn't safe for me. As long as we were in South Carolina we'd be spending the rest of our lives running. Those men would never stop hunting us, especially me. This is when I realized what a mixed blessing having powerful ancestors was."

Now the scene showed Gizelle leaving her group to set off on her own. A few of the members did everything they could to stop her, but there was a steadfast determination in the set of Gizelle's jaw. There was nothing the people could do.

"I knew I had to make it to Florida. I heard there were tribes down there that would take you in if you joined them against the white folk. I knew I wasn't much of a fighter but I had my mother's gift. Whenever I called the spirits, whether it was to spin a story or stage a defense, the spirits came. Any decent medicine woman would notice it in me right away, so I bet on that, and that's exactly what happened. I didn't know I was in Florida by the time I made it here."

The young woman, filthy and frail, slugged into the clearing in the darkness of night. She gathered some berries, then climbed the tree using what looked like the last bit of her energy. She finally rested on a sturdy branch high in the tree, the same branch that was now ablaze with shimmering orange flames.

"That tree we just came from, that was the tree that I tried to hide in. I was so tired, hadn't eaten in a couple of days, and gathered what I could from the surroundings to last me a while just to rest. The thick leaves protected me for a couple days until a band of hunters from one of the Seminole tribes out here found me and took me hostage."

"That is terrible," Marsha sighed, "you escaped just to be taken captive again!"

"Oh but baby, remember, I had spirits on my side! They took me right to their chief and council members, one of which was a medicine woman. Sure enough, she saw the power in me right away." Gizelle had a glimmer in her eyes as she wove this new turn in the tale.

"I tried to strike a bargain with her, said I would help them any way I could if the tribe took me in."

The scene now showed the young woman being led into the center of a large gathering, with several decorated elders sitting behind a fire pit. The eldest woman on the council stood and addressed the man who appeared to be the chief. The village people stood along the exposed sides of the pavilion. She could hear soft drumming as if it was far in the distance. The people themselves were mute, but Marsha could see their mouths moving. She imagined what they were saying—the negotiations, translated from language to language. The tribe's people were a mosaic of shades, with a few distinctive features indicating a shared bloodline. Marsha assumed many had family members who were refugees at one point, and joined together to keep themselves strong against a common enemy. She imagined this connection inspired their grace towards her great-grandmother.

"The woman spoke. At the time I couldn't understand the language, but they had a young translator present. He smiled at me and waved his hands. They knew where I came from, and other members of their tribe came from similar places. They said I could stay there as long as I wanted, and if I wanted to help them, they would accept it."

The eldest woman stood, tall and magnificent in her adornments, and opened her arms to the young woman before her.

"Now the only way I could truly be a member of the tribe was if I married into it, and that meant they had to find someone suitable for me, their new oracle. Luckily, one such man had just become eligible for marriage. When they brought him out, I recognized him as the head of the hunting party that found me. I had never seen somebody so tall and chiseled ... But the thing that struck me the most was his skin. His skin was darker red.

Deeper black. He wasn't like the other hunters of his tribe. Swallowtail was a warrior, a good one, but he was also a teacher, and spoke many languages. He knew math and astronomy, architecture and how to live with the forest. And you know what the best thing was? He had a heart of gold to match that mind of his. I think you have to in order to be a good warrior. You need to know exactly why you're doing the things you gotta do. I learned that from my father.

"They paired us together, gave us our own chickee—that was their name for a house—well within their land, and set us on this plot to live. At first, our union was political. But it didn't take me very long to love that man, or for him to love me. A lot of other women in my situation were not as lucky. I learned the language and started helping the tribe navigate the relations with the people settling around us. Around that time, the white folk were hunting Natives like rabbits. Our only hope of survival was to stick together. I learned that most of the community wasn't from the same tribe in the first place. They had traveled from all over and banded together after their tribes were disbanded or hunted. Swallowtail himself was from Louisiana. When the relations with the Americans were simmering down, he built us this cabin right here, and a few months later, we found out I was pregnant with my first child—well, first child conceived out of love."

Marsha looked away from the story now, right at Gizelle. The sweet reminiscence in her elder's eyes filled Marsha up with something she couldn't explain. A belonging, a sense of self, an understanding of who she was. She grabbed the old woman's hand and leaned on her shoulder, and Gizelle smiled, and rested her head against Marsha's.

"We had three more children just like that. All out of love. All raised in a tribe that loved them. We were heavily involved in the tribe's politics. One day, they came to us when it was time to decide if we were going to go to war with the white folk again. They had fought and lost the Seminole wars well before I got there, but because of the work of our medicine women, we were able to stay here on our land. We didn't need to fight. But I knew that our safety was fragile, especially for the descendants of an escaped slave. I heard stories from the Natives that adopted me, about how their ancestors gave their whole tribe gifts to ensure their success with whatever endeavor they set out upon. So I went to the medicine woman, and I asked if she would teach me the ritual so that I could give my children the same. It took some convincing, but eventually she said she would. The ritual hadn't been done in a very long time, so it took a while to prepare and make sure it was done right."

Marsha and her father listened intently. The visions had drifted away, and were replaced by the gray shimmer of the moonlit forest. Gizelle spoke directly to them. No story or crafted vision could relay the seriousness in her eyes.

"That night, I took each of my babies to the medicine woman and told her what I wanted for them—to see, to hear, to feel, and to know their history. Their story. If something happened to me or Swallowtail, I never wanted them to forget the power from which they came, and the magic that was woven into their DNA. And most of all, I wanted them to be able to protect themselves if that story was ever threatened. I wanted them each to have all four gifts, but I guess something got lost in translation, and instead, they each got one. Your great-grandpa was about four or five at the time, and my youngest, Lanae, was born only a few weeks before. We had to wait years before we started to see the effects of the ritual. Around the time your great-grandfather started to display his clairvoyance, all of the time I'd spent trying to forget my life in South Carolina caught up to me, and my memory started drifting away. I think the medicine woman saw it going before anyone, and that's why she agreed to do the ritual in the first place.

"I thought I taught them enough. I thought the stories made it clear," Gizelle said, almost as if talking to herself, then shook her head in disappointment.

"These gifts were intended to be together, so that's how they work best. They're charged and strengthened by familial bonds. But if you don't use them, they fester like an illness or bad habit. Like what you and Tre are experiencing right now." Gizelle nodded her head towards Marvin. "To me, it's an easy fix. Just need to stay close. And united. As long as we do that, the gifts take care of themselves. But the farther we are apart, the more likely we are to suffer. The blessing can easily become a curse."

"So, when we moved away, we kind of messed everything up huh," Marvin realized, shame in the thick of his voice.

"No, baby, that wasn't the only thing," Gizelle comforted. "Like I said earlier, the poison had been building up. A person can be far away from somebody and close as can be. That's what's going on with Chinara's line. She and her daughter are tight as a knot, and that line has the strongest connection to their gifts so far, but they still come up short. I can scream at Chinara and it's like she only hears a whisper."

Gizelle widened her eyes in subtle annoyance, then smiled at Marsha.

"Now Marsha here, something about her curiosity and wit sparked the gift in this line to reemerge, stronger than ever. Spirits must've seen it and noticed that maybe she could be the one who pulled all the pieces together."

Marsha smiled and grabbed her elbows across her chest. It was humbling to know her gift was strong, but intimidating to realize how much responsibility came with it.

XIII

"It didn't start with you, Marvin. It started here." Gizelle suddenly looked off into the forest again.

The voices of a mob rose in the distance, and Marsha scooted closer to her father on the steps.

"It's okay child, remember, this is just a vision. They're not really there and they're not really gonna get you. Just watch what happens."

The figure of Michael Swallowtail Sr. burst through the forestline. He looked pale and ghostly, not only from fear, but also because of the shaded transparency of his form in the vision. He ran right towards the trio and before Marsha could move aside, he bolted up the stairs, passing right through them into the house. Marsha followed him inside and found him rummaging through a drawer full of papers. Gizelle and Marvin hurried in seconds later. The figure was throwing papers all about, looking for something. One of the documents fell to the floor right at Marsha's feet. It was Aunt Marybell's birth certificate. A few seconds later, he found whatever he was looking for. He held it to the light to confirm, and there it was. The missing deed to the land. Michael ran over to a vanity that must've been his wife's and emptied the contents of a small blue box.

Sapphire, Marsha said to herself. *It's fire resistant.*

Michael Swallowtail Sr. folded the deed small enough to fit in the box, and then went to run back out of the cabin, but stopped, as if he had an idea. He picked up the birth certificate then disappeared through the door.

"Come on, we gotta get to the tree quick. Y'all think y'all can wish yourself back there? We'll miss it if we try to run."

Marsha looked at her father, who looked back at her, and they both nodded. They closed their eyes and imagined. Marsha thought about how magnificent it looked when sitting under its canopy, gazing into branches that seemed to infinitely climb towards the sky. Marvin thought back to how the deeply ridged bark gently held him when he was a boy cradled in its branches.

Before they knew it, they opened their eyes and were back at the tree. Michael Swallowtail Sr. was sprinting towards it just as they arrived. Marsha heard the mob's hateful voices getting louder and saw the light from the torches approaching the treeline. Her great-grandfather flew past her and found an eye in the tree, opposite the side where the burning branch was. But this time, the fire was absent. A glimmer of hope sent goosebumps through Marsha's body, but Gizelle's words rang in her ears. "That branch had to burn."

Michael stuffed the sapphire box in the tree's eye, covered it with a thick layer of leaves and branches, then closed his eyes and whispered a prayer.

Suddenly, voices broke from the trailhead. Michael ran to the other side of the tree to confront the mob at last. He took out the second piece of paper, the birth certificate, and held it up with his hands in a surrendering action.

"Michael Cole Swallowtail," a voice said in a deep, country accent. "You are under arrest for assault and battery and evading arrest. All you need to do is hand over that deed, and we'll make sure that you're protected and taken care of."

Michael Sr. smiled at this, a chilling chuckle of a man who had already accepted his fate. He took out a match and set the paper on fire.

"Damn you!" The sheriff cursed. "It is my civil decree that Michael Cole Swallowtail be handed over to the people so that they may fairly judge his fate!"

Michael threw the paper on the tree and the branch quickly caught fire. Then he walked slowly towards the mob, his silhouette darkening in the bright torchlight. Before Marsha could see what happened next, the whole scene vanished.

Marsha stood speechless.

Gizelle started again.

"I wasn't in my right mind long enough to teach him, so my son thought that self sacrifice was the only way to save the tree. He didn't know the spirits or their power. He didn't know his own. But he could see one thing about the future clear as day. He could see that the tree would grow strong. That we would be okay. And that's something even I didn't understand. Think of a tomato plant. They grow all of these branches when they're young. Some grow big and tall, stretching up to the sun. Some grow just in case the strong ones don't survive. And some grow close to the bottom of the plant. In nature, those are trampled or eaten by animals to eventually become part of the soil. Part of the grander ecosystem. Part of what feeds and cares for the plant for the rest of its life. Now, you can keep them on, but it's likely that it will affect the fruit later down the road. My son made himself that branch that day. And because of that, the gifts were able to be passed down to all of the generations. Whatever he said to that tree when he put that sapphire box in there, whatever ritual was completed when he lit the branch on fire, made this tree something sacred. A shrine just for our family. And we need to make sure we're keeping it safe and protected."

As she spoke, the branch on the tree became fully engulfed in the flames, and the three Swallowtails stood together watching it burn. Through her own conflicting emotions, Marsha understood now what that branch meant to her family. What it meant to Gizelle. It represented all of the things Gizelle escaped when she arrived in Florida, all of the emotions and trauma and fear that she had carried all her life. It represented the ways each of her descendants had all taken on her pain whether they knew it or not. Gizelle was right. It needed to burn. The fire seemed to have a consciousness in the way it consumed the branch without jumping or spitting an ember to any other leaf. With a large crack, the flame fell to the ground bringing what remained of the branch with it, where the moisture and the soggy Florida ground eventually put it out completely.

PART III
CONNECTED

XIV

Knock, knock, knock!

Marvin creaked open his daughter's door just as the sun broke through the treeline behind their home.

Marsha groggily turned out of her sheets and rubbed the sleep from her eyes. "What time is it?" she mumbled with a yawn.

Marvin checked a fake watch on his arm, then peeked out the window pretending to read the sunlight.

"I'd say about 7:30 A.M. ..."

"Ughhhhhhh," Marsha moaned, plopping back down onto her bed.

"Don't get too comfy. I need your help with something."

Marsha groaned. "It's Sunday. Isn't it supposed to be a day of rest? Plus, you have two other children who weren't up with you all night in the Traverse."

"Well, I was thinking, since your family tree project is due this week and your gift is a little more tuned in than mine, maybe you'd wanna come with me and Uncle Tre to help look for this deed. But, I guess not ..." Marvin shrugged and slowly turned to leave, waiting to see if his lure worked. Marsha immediately sat straight up.

"Let's go!"

"Yeah, that's what I thought," Marvin joked at his success. "The only thing we've got to figure out how to do is get on the land. The city still has the entryway locked up."

"I think I have an idea about that," Marsha admitted.

"Yesterday, while I was waiting for Cleo to go to Aunt Chi's, I had a daytime vision. It was the first time it happened but I was sitting on the park bench when the whole thing turned to forest. There was something interesting about one of the trail entrances at the back of the park over there. Grandma Gizelle was flying over me in her bird form so I wonder if she was trying to tell me something. Do you think we should start there?"

"At this point, I agree with anything you think is the right way to go," Marvin kissed his daughter's forehead. "You ready?"

Marsha jumped out of bed to get dressed.

"Give me ten minutes!"

They arrived at the park just past eight as Uncle Tre was pulling into the parking lot.

"You look a lot better," he said to Marvin as he closed his car door. "Hey Marsha, good to see you again."

"Hey, Uncle Tre," Marsha responded then leaned in for a hug.

Tre awkwardly extended his hand to Marvin as if he didn't know how to greet his brother. Marvin shook it for a moment then pulled him in for a quick, uncomfortable hug. Rebuilding their relationship would have to start somewhere.

"So, um ... how you feeling today?" Tre asked to break the discomfort.

"Still a little sore, but I'm here, and I'm grateful. Come on, Marsha's gonna take the lead today."

Marsha scanned the treeline in the spot she had seen the day before.

"There it is! Follow me!"

She led them to a terribly overgrown trailhead just at the forest edge. After pulling aside a few branches and stepping over a few small bushy plants, the old trail made itself clear. The trio walked in silence for a while through the dense, verdant path until it opened into a loblolly pine forest.

"Why don't you go ahead while I talk to your uncle? Not too far though, I want to keep you in my view. We'll be right behind you."

Marsha obeyed then started off into the woods. For a moment both men watched her.

"That's a really good kid you got there. All of them are. You're truly blessed, brother," Tre said finally.

"Yeah, she is. I am. We are."

"So what's up with this deed, man? You said you know where it is?" Marvin could tell Tre was starting to get uncomfortable with the weird lack of tension or animosity between them. He spent the entire morning trying to figure out how this part would go. How this conversation would occur. There was so much to unpack between them, and he knew one talk wouldn't be enough. So he decided to start with what mattered most.

"When you were doing all that gambling and stuff, it wasn't really gambling was it? You knew the outcome didn't you?"

Tre looked around him suspiciously.

"Aye, what are you trying to say, man? I ain't never stole from nobody or nothing like that."

"Tre, we are in the middle of the forest at 8 A.M. on a Sunday. No one who would be looking for you like that is awake right now, let alone out here."

Tre nodded and tilted his head from side to side acknowledging Marvin's point.

"Be honest with me. You be knowing things. Things that nobody else can know. That's how you came up with the money to open the bar, isn't it ... and why you felt confident betting it all away that day after Dad's funeral?"

Tre stopped walking and looked at Marvin very seriously.

"What do you know?" he asked.

"I know that I know things too. But in a different way than you. I see things happen before they happen. I saw Mom and Dad's death. And I saw your diagnosis. And Marsha, she knows things just the same. I'm thinking it runs in the family. So, just tell me. You know things too." Marvin opened his palms wide to show he had nothing to hide, no blade behind his intent.

Tre chuckled to himself and turned to walk again, Marvin following his lead.

"Yeah," Tre said finally. "I do. For the longest, I thought I was crazy because I really believed it. Everyone already had a whole lot to say about the choices I made, so can you imagine me telling them I only chose that way because of voices in my head? I mean, it's not even voices. An idea just like ... pops in my head and it turns out to be something. Like that day of the city council meeting. Everyone's been talking about how I stormed in, but what about the fact that they didn't even tell us! I didn't see it in none of them neighborhood papers. I just knew. Something told me to go to the library and next thing I know, I'm barging in on a city council meeting where they're talking about our land. Plans to develop it and destroy it. I wasn't prepared and everybody thought I was crazy, but imagine if they knew that I knew how I knew to go there?"

"I don't think you're crazy. As a matter of fact, I know you're not." Marvin continued to tell Tre about everything he learned had transpired in the past day. From their lost, now found, older cousin Gezie, to the new information about their family's gifts and history.

"So you're telling me that those ideas that pop into my head are some sort of spiritual gift?"

"That's exactly what I'm telling you. I have one that lets me see things, so does Marsha.

"And Chinara?" Tre asked.

"She hears stuff."

"What about Dad? Or your other children?"

"See, that's the thing. Grandma Gizelle told us that there were rules. We're supposed to stay close, remember those who came before us, and not hold any grudges, hate, jealousy, or anything like that against other family members. If we don't follow the rules, our gifts weaken and become undetectable. And if it gets too bad," Marvin looked at Tre. "Well, we can get sick."

The twins stopped to exchange a look that said more than their words ever could. It spoke of suspicions and understandings, guilt and acceptance, realization and redemption. Marvin stared at himself through his brother's gaze. He saw the same square head, the same chiseled features, the same wide nose, and the same righteous determination. Tre was his living mirror, reflecting the best and worst parts of him. Perhaps for the first time in his life, Marvin recognized the real gift they shared. There was so much more that needed to be said. But for now, the pair walked on in silence.

"Look, before you say anything else," Tre started, causing Marvin to hold his breath. He had no idea what Tre had gone through while his family was experiencing so much the day before, so he let his brother talk uninterrupted.

"I ... I don't know how to explain how sorry I am about how everything went down yesterday. If I would've known it'd cause you so much stress ... I don't know, maybe I would've gone about things in a different way. Either way, it shouldn't have taken that. You're my brother. I'm not gonna lie, that scared me to see you hurt like that. You know, down and out." Tre shook his head at himself, disappointed.

"But I had a lot of time to think last night. I have asked you for so much in the past couple of months, shoot, our whole lives. But I can't remember one time I helped you with something, or had your back. I can't even remember the last time I called just to see how you and the family were doing. Still, whenever I needed anything or dug myself into a hole I couldn't get out of, you were there. I expected you to be. I assumed because not only are you my brother but you're just the type of person that comes through. Every time. And I chose to repay you by asking you for even more. Ha. Sure is a piss poor way to show someone my appreciation." Tre took a deep sigh.

"I can't believe how selfish I was. Moving is one thing, but a whole liver, a whole surgery. I didn't even think about it until I saw you laying there on the ground. I was so scared. I couldn't move, couldn't think. Dr. Coleman had to call 911 'cause I ... I just couldn't. I was so terrified at the thought of losing you. I was thinking about what I would tell Yonna. What I would tell your kids ... how I am not prepared to be even half of the man you are."

Marvin tried to interject here. He didn't like hearing Tre talk about himself without his unbearably charming confidence, but Tre stopped him.

"Just hear me out, man, damn."

The twins shot the same *Who are you talking to?* look at each other at the same exact time. After a split second of tension, they both chuckled.

"Honestly Marvin, as much as we haven't gotten along, I don't know what I would do if I lost you for real. Yesterday, I saw you do for your boy and your family what our father wasn't able to do for us ... I'm not willing to risk what you've built. Not when I've had so many other chances to pull my own life out of the trash can. I told Dr. Coleman to go ahead and put me on the donor list. If it's meant to be, it will be. Since my condition is getting worse, I might have a match within the year. Dr. Coleman said it was a good time to try chemo to see if we can shrink the tumor and maybe by then I won't even need a transplant. Either way, I couldn't ask you to do something to jeopardize your family. I won't ask you."

Marvin tried to hide his smile at the irony. He opened his mouth to say something, but before he could, Tre started talking again.

"Look, I don't need you to say anything or try to negate my decision. Just let me have this one."

Marvin raised his eyebrows high and nodded in acceptance. He would let Tre have this moment, but he had already made a decision of his own.

"Over here!" Marsha called, breaking up the moment at the perfect time. The twins turned to Marsha standing at the threshold of the trail with a tapestry of thick green grasses and dogfennel layered behind her. The threshold itself was framed by two massive cranberry hibiscus bushes.

"That's crazy," Marsha said as they approached her. Marvin and Tre exchanged another look.

"What's crazy?" Marvin asked.

"Y'all are really twins. Like … same height, same skin, same beard … I couldn't tell y'all apart until you got close enough for me to see Daddy's birthmark! Anyway, come on! I think that's the tree." Glowing with excitement, Marsha turned around and ran into the landscape towards an old oak tree.

Tre and Marvin shared a laugh.

By the time the twins made it through the clearing, Marsha was already standing at the base of the tree holding something high above her head. It gleamed at Marvin for a split second as the sun hit the object just right. Then, it unveiled itself—a small, deep blue box.

"It was in the eye under a bunch of leaves, just like we saw in the Traverse!"

Marvin's chest swelled as Tre opened the box. This time, anxiety wasn't the presiding emotion. Hope was.

XV

THAT EVENING, YONNA AND AUNT MARYBELL CALLED FOR a big Sunday dinner at Aunt Marybell's house. All of their friends and family were invited, from Mrs. Loretta and Ms. Bee, to Dr. Coleman and his wife. Marsha was most excited for Cleo and her parents to be introduced as members of the family. Even Aunt Chi and Mr. Kwe were invited, despite their strained relationship with Aunt Marybell. There was so much food that it reminded Marsha of Thanksgiving. Candied yams, mac and cheese, Cornish hens, homemade dinner rolls, stuffed fish, and crab croquettes. The house was filled with the sounds and smells of a family reunited and ready to eat.

Marsha was elated. She had never been around so much of her family before. Everywhere she turned she found a familiar face, some who knew her better than she knew herself. She was breathing with the type of clarity that only comes when you are completely comfortable, completely free to just ... be.

Still, after everything that occurred that weekend, there was one thing still heavy on Marsha's heart. After a running start, she slid into the kitchen and found Aunt Marybell pulling her legendary pound cake out of the oven.

"Do you need any help Aunt Marybell?"

"Oh no baby, thank you for asking though! That was very sweet of you."

Marybell set the cake on the cooling rack then spun around to turn down the pot of simmering greens.

"Thank you for doing all of this. It smells amazing! And it's so cool to have all of the family here."

"Oh, of course baby, it's been so long since we've had this many people in here, let alone family. I almost forgot how good it felt."

After recovering the pot and wiping her hands, she tossed an old hand towel over her shoulder then leaned a hip on the counter facing her great-niece, waiting for whatever came next.

"I have a question," Marsha proclaimed. "But I'm not sure how you're gonna take it."

"I'm sure you do," Aunt Marybell replied, one eyebrow raised.

Marsha rocked back and forth on her heels, contemplating how the question would go over with her aunt. As soon as the courage overcame her, she blurted it out before apprehension kept her silent any longer.

"What ever happened with you and Aunt Chinara?"

Aunt Marybell nodded as if she expected this moment to arise.

"Well, I guess it makes sense that you'd want to know after all of this. All I can say is, we had our differences because of how we felt when we experienced our gifts. When we were younger, our gifts were stronger and less controlled, which made us more sensitive to each other's experiences. I imagine that's where it started. I can't tell you exactly what happened. It was so long ago. But I'll tell you something I've learned over the years. One of my biggest flaws has always been how I isolate. When something goes wrong or gets uncomfortable, into my little world I go. During that time, it was my world with your Uncle VanDyke, with him being a musician and all. Our lives were so full of music and travel. My family and our history was complicated, and hurtful at times. It became something I thought about less and less, until I didn't think about it at all. After a while, I guess I got so used to being apart. But I miss her. I've missed her for a long time. I'd be lying if I said I haven't been trying to imagine the right thing to say when she arrives later on."

"Well, how's 'hey' for a start?"

The voice came from the threshold on the other side of the kitchen. Standing there, under the doorway, Aunt Chi smiled big with eyes full of tears.

"Hey there, little bird," she said, facing Marsha. "Can you get this bag off me, please?" Marsha took the bag and smelled it, pretending she wasn't completely tuned in to what was happening with the two women.

"Mmm mm," Marsha cooed, letting the savory-spice smell of jambalaya tickle her nose. "I can't wait to eat this."

Her great-aunts ignored her, completely enthralled in their own reunion.

"You look good, girl," Aunt Chi said, still holding back her tears.

"And so do you," Marybell responded.

"Mary. I—" Chinara started after another long moment. But before she could finish her sentence, Marybell rushed over and pulled Chinara into her arms, hugging her close. Surprised, it took Chinara a second before she settled into the hug. Marsha heard the knock of Mr. Kwe's cane as he rounded the corner and was stopped in his tracks as if he could see what was going on.

"Marsha, would you mind walking me outside? I'd like to get some fresh air, and don't want to go for a swim in my fresh linen suit." He smiled and winked, then led Marsha out so the women could have their time.

The family enjoyed a beautiful evening of food, storytelling, and communion. After dinner, Marsha and Cleo practiced their presentation of their family tree project in front of everyone. At the end they got a standing ovation. Mrs. Loretta was in tears and even Jeremy was impressed by the story. Or at least he acted like he was.

After they were all full on dessert and the afternoon football game was over, Marvin stood and cleared his throat, calling everyone to attention.

"These past few weeks have truly been transformative for our family. We made some mistakes, learned many, many lessons, and most importantly, we grew. We grew as individuals and as a family itself, and now these roots seem stronger than ever before. Well, all of that hard work has proved to be important on many fronts. Today, with the help of my daughter Marsha, Tre and I were able to locate this."

He unfolded the delicate parchment and held it up to the family.

"This paper right here is the beneficiary deed to 7310 Live Oak Drive. It states that the property's forty-seven acres of land legally belong to the descendants of Michael Cole Swallowtail Sr.: Michael Cole Swallowtail Jr., Chinara Lanae Swallowtail, Marybell Gizelle Swallowtail, and Marvin Cole Swallowtail."

Marsha smiled from ear to ear as she watched her family erupt in excited discussion. Aunt Marybell grabbed her hand under the table and squeezed as if to brace herself. Marsha squeezed back and looked up to find tears in her aunt's eyes.

"I don't believe it," Aunt Marybell whispered.

"Now, I wanna be clear," Marvin continued, "This fight is not over. We still need to go down to the county clerk and make it official. But I want to make sure when we go down there, we have a plan. We're going against some big businesses that can make a lot of money for the city, so we need to come correct, united, and be prepared to fight."

His reminder of the path ahead of them dulled the excitement to a lull.

"I have a suggestion for the time being," Aunt Marybell spoke up. "There are only two of us living that are listed on the deed, and too many hands in the pot can become an issue. One of us has lived on the edge of that land for just about forever. I think it makes most sense to leave it to her. Our matriarch. The one who tried to keep us all together, brought us all back together, plus some," she winked at Gezie, "and never held a grudge in her heart. All in favor, say 'Chi.'"

Every voice in the room said "Chi," filling Chinara's eyes with glossy tears.

"Oh stop it now, y'all gon' make my liner run. I'll put my name down on that little paper as long as y'all stop all this crying."

"Dear," Mr. Kwe said gently, "My ears are telling me the only person crying is you."

Chinara's jaw dropped in fake betrayal and the home filled with laughter once more.

XVI

"AND THAT IS HOW OUR ERITREAN FAMILY TOOK root here, in America," Samira said proudly wrapping up their presentation. "Now, Senai will pass out a traditional Eritrean dish, kicha fit fit." The class broke out in applause, cheering loudly as Senai navigated the aisles between desks.

Nerves suddenly overtook Marsha's excitement.

Sensing Marsha's change in energy, Cleo tapped her arm.

"Hey, you okay?"

"I don't know. How are we supposed to go after that? That was amazing!"

"Girl, c'mon! Samira and Senai could have gotten up here and said five words and the class would still act like this just because they brought food."

"Well, then we should have brought the rest of Aunt Chi's jambalaya!" Marsha whispered back.

Cleo rolled her eyes.

"Their project was great, and so is ours! Our family is awesome, and so is our story. Especially the part where we find out we're cousins! They're gonna love that!" Cleo's words comforted Marsha. By the time the class settled down, Marsha was ready.

The girls took their spot at the front of the classroom together. Marsha shot Cleo a final look, and Cleo winked.

"A week and a half ago I sat at a new desk, at a new school, in a new town. I was more frustrated than nervous, mainly, because in the weeks before, the life that I had lived until now changed in the blink of an eye. A week and a half ago I sat at my desk on the outskirts of class trying to make myself invisible, but was interrupted." Marsha darted her eyes between Cleo and Samira, who both giggled quietly.

"Then, Ms. Arbor shook my reality by offering a new perspective, one that claims knowledge of self starts from knowing where you come from. You see, a week and a half ago, if you asked about my family, I would tell you of my wonderfully perfect older sister, my impossibly annoying big brother, and my baby brother who is the sweetest, most lovable soul. I'd tell you about Aunt Marybell and Uncle VanDyke who watch us over the summers, and I'd tell you about my parents and how mad I was at them for moving me here to Ocala, where they're from. That's about all I'd say, because a week and a half ago, that's about all I really knew. I thought I knew myself ... inquisitive, kind, hated birds for a good reason ... I knew the lengths that I would go to protect myself, and the ways I would fight for the people I love. But to know where I came from? That started at Mrs. Loretta's shop—a community staple where women can go for everything they didn't know they needed. It was there that I was first told that Swallowtails in Ocala go together like honey in the beehive. So, inspired by Mrs. Loretta's storytelling beauty salon and the oral traditions of our ancestors, Cleo and I put together the fairytale of our family. Each event in the story is as true or whimsical as you wish to believe. As you listen, each character will unfold itself, and will be added to the family tree behind us. I hope you enjoy it."

And with that, Cleo stepped forward and began.

"Once upon a time, there were two girls destined to be together. They were bound by blood, but separated by blight."

XVII

OKAY, I GUESS BIRDS AREN'T THAT BAD ... *at least not all of them. Sandhill cranes should still keep their distance, especially if I'm holding a rattail. And I guess Ocala isn't that bad either. Okay, fine. I love Ocala. I love the plants and the sunny weather. I love my school and my new best friend ... cousin ... frousin! But most of all, I love my family and how much I have learned about myself by learning our history here. I see myself in every corner of this town and I realize just how much of me was crafted by those who came before. Oh, trust me ... I still have questions. TONS of questions. When will my siblings get their gifts? Have they been hiding them this whole time like Uncle Tre? What happened to Swallowtail, Grandma Gizelle's husband? How long will this peace between my father and uncle last? Most importantly, what will we make of those forty-seven acres now that it's back in our hands for good?*

Whatever we decide, I know God has a plan for me and the rest of my family. A plan to unpack these mysteries that we didn't know were so important to solve, and rebuild bridges that were burned to ashes. I'm ready.

Marissa Lanae
Jeremy Cole
Jacob Cole
Michael Cole "Tre" Swallowtail III
Marvin and Yonna
Michael Cole Swallowtail Jr. and Sarah
Aunt Marybell and Uncle VanDyke
Millie
Michael Cole Swallowtail Sr.
Gizelle

Marsha Claire
Cleo Bell
Gezie
Lil' Marv
Aunt Chinara & Kwe
Lanae
Winona
Swallowtail

QUESTIONS FOR DISCUSSION

1. When Marsha and Cleo found the WANTED listing about Michael Cole Swallowtail Sr., Cleo's first reaction was, "something here doesn't sound right." What details from the article do you think made Cleo feel that way? What ideas do the article expose about the law enforcement system in Florida during the early 1900s?

2. When the enslaved people in the United States of America were finally emancipated, one of their first duties was to identify themselves and "choose" a last name. Some chose to take the name of their former enslaver, such as Williams and Jackson; some chose the name of their occupation, like Forrester; and others decided to pick a name for themselves, like Freeman. What do the surnames Cleo shared say about her family's ideologies? What details from the story show how these ideologies appear to have shaped Cleo?

3. Many members of the Swallowtail family are named after relatives: Gezie is named for Gizelle and there are three generations of Michael Coles. Why do you think the Swallowtails pass names down from generation to generation?

4. In her assessment of *Bronze Star*, Marsha wonders why so many stories about Black people are about "overcoming something terrible in order to be the first to do something." Yonna explains that more joyful stories are often passed down through oral tradition. How do you celebrate the fullness of your cultural heritage? What steps can people take to tell cultural stories with care?

5. *Why the Birds Fly Back* is organized in parts: CAGED, CALLED, and CONNECTED. Why do you think the parts are titled accordingly: Who is *caged*, and why? Who is *called*, and to what? Who's *connected*, and how?

6. Throughout the novel, Yonna battles with silent guilt because she did not share her thoughts about her husband's decision to lie to their children. Think about your relationships with your family, friends, and loved ones. Do you think you are responsible for warning them about potential bad decisions? Where do you draw the line between supporting their decisions and helping them make good ones?

7. When Marvin met his father Mikey in the Traverse, Mikey told him, "Yeah, your past is on me, rightfully so. But your present and your future, Marvin, that's on you, son." What does Mikey mean by this statement? How does Marvin respond to this piece of advice?

8. Gizelle Swallowtail explains that the gifts she gave her descendants work best when the family is united and the family members use their gifts regularly. What message does this send about how we can show up in our own families and communities? What gifts were you given and how can you use them to preserve and strengthen your communities?

ABOUT THE AUTHOR

Akosua LauraJeanne Faye Harvey is an educator, writer, and medium whose work explores the intersections of ancestry, culture, identity, and community. A passionate storyteller, Akosua channels her experiences as a Black woman and educator to challenge, uplift, and inspire. With a background in physics and science literacy, her unique perspective aims to blend intellect and artistry in a way that is accessible to young minds, offering a voice that is both authentic and impactful. Akosua's works are celebrations of resilience, creativity, and the transformative and healing power of words.

ABOUT STIRRED STORIES

The same stories have repeatedly been told. We're here to stir that up.

We believe that in order to create a truly just society, the stories we consume must be diverse and equitable. That's why we center authenticity and diversity in everything we do, from the books we publish to how we publish them. In short, we're publishing for a better tomorrow.

Follow along with us at www.stirredstories.com.